A. M. KHERBASH

Lesath

ISBN: 978-1-7338854-1-6

eBook ISBN: 978-1-7338854-3-0

www.amkherbash.com

For my husband

Lesasth:

(Upsilon Scorpii) a star located in the "stinger" of the southern zodiac constellation of Scorpius, the scorpion. The name is said to have come from the Arabic word *las'a*: a poisonous bite or sting.

PROLOGUE

"I'm here, Ory—that place I heard of.

"Here's hoping this time the phone's mic will hold up and won't quit on me in the middle of recording like it did last time, leaving me with about twenty minutes of dead silence. And this was supposed to be a refurbished model. But it seems to be working alright, and this log is just between us, so hopefully last time was just a hiccup.

"Anyhow, I could try and explain how I got here: you won't find this place on any map or GIS—at least not the ones I tried. Maps list this place as a dense forest, and satellite images reveal nothing but blurred photos. I guess someone wants to keep the area dark. But if you can find a map that's at least a decade old… there's a place called Duncastor, just north of Palais Gris. There used to be a seafood cannery operating in the area that's now closed off and left to decay. Find the cannery, hike a few miles up the unmarked mountain path behind it, and you won't be far off from where I am now. Granted, this is my second day in the area: there's no reception here, and it's easy to get lost if you're not paying attention.

"Sorry about the scratching noise. I needed both hands for a steep climb just now, and the mic's cable keeps rubbing against the collar. Alright, I just got to higher grounds and—

"Wait—I think I see it. There's actually something there. It's far off, but from where I'm standing, I can make out a U-shaped building tucked in this mountain forest. Imagine a cul-de-sac made up of rocky walls and trees surrounding this grand, palace-sized building. The rolling fog makes it all seem ghostly. I don't know if it's as abandoned as it looks from here, but it's quite the view."

"Hey, it's me again. Had to stop recording for a while and play it back just to make sure everything's working. Plus, I thought it's better if I stayed quiet and kept my eyes peeled. On the way down, I passed by an area with wires strung between trees, maybe meant to trip someone, if not trigger an alarm or a trap. The place is set up with such subtle traps. I'm getting closer to the building now, and the grounds here are covered in glass shards, in case you're wondering about that crunching under my boots—those aren't just a few broken bottles littering the ground. I thought I'd only find an abandoned building here, but someone really made an effort to make the area inhospitable… Granted, I didn't come across any electric fences or 'Keep Out!' signs. Which begs the question: who are they trying to deter here? The local wildlife? Squatters? Nosy amateur reporters like yours truly?"

"I'm switching to whispering now: I just found out I'm not the only one here. There's a guy about thirty feet away, and—I don't think you can catch that, but he's mumbling something into this black brick of a device that he's holding close to his mouth—too big to be a phone—a walkie-talkie maybe, or a handheld recorder. Yeah, a recorder—I don't hear any static. Anyway, he's just squatting there, almost hunched over the device in his hand, talking to it non-stop. And—is he barefoot?

"Shit!

"Oh, crap, he must have heard me!

"He's gone now. He just stopped talking all of a sudden, and I had to duck out of view before he could turn around and see me. I'm keeping my voice down; I'd rather be the one sneaking up on others than the other way round. Although he does kinda stand out in his outfit: some dark grey or denim jumpsuit with a reflective orange armband, and… I think he wasn't wearing any shoes. I'm not sure—that's not possible, not with all that broken glass littering the grounds. I don't know. It's weird, now that I think of it.

"What do you think, Ory? Think there might be some truth to those rumors? I don't know. Maybe I'm on edge for no reason. I'm a little sleep-deprived from last night. I say night, but it was only four hours of proper darkness pinched between long stretches of daylight. I parked the truck in some hidden spot, but I don't think I'll trek all the way down if I could—"

CHAPTER I

It was cold. Greg huddled and drew the blankets about him, bringing them as close to his ears as possible without muffling his nose and mouth.

Something stung his left temple. He touched it and was puzzled when his fingers registered a soft texture. But the palm he pressed to his brow reassured him it was only a square of gauze held by two bandage strips. His eyes were open now, though it took him a few moments to process the fact that he was lying in an iron bed in an unfamiliar room.

It was a dim room, with little to identify it apart from its bare white walls, pale linoleum floor, and a row of narrow windows.

A cursory glance under the blanket showed him that his clothes had been replaced by an inadequate, green, papery gown, which suggested the possibility he was hospitalized, though he had no memory of an incident or anything that might have led to him being here.

The last thing he remembered was hiking up a mountain path to investigate something; any subsequent events were lost to him, and his attempt at trying to recall them was met with a blank wall.

He grew restless and wanted to get up and walk around to jump-start his lagging memory, as well as reassure himself that nothing was broken. The cold air—along with a vague sense of modesty—gave him pause to wrap the wool blanket cloak-like around his shoulders before slowly stepping towards the narrow windows.

"Windows" was perhaps a generous term for the two slits carved deep within the thick wall, which allowed sheets of orange sunlight to slant through but offered no view of the outside, regardless of how Greg tilted and shifted his head.

Someone cleared their throat behind him, and he turned to find a nurse who somehow managed to come in without making a sound and now stood there, jotting down something on a clipboard.

"Where am I?" he asked in a hoarse voice.

She kept on writing, her eyes cast down, allowing him to observe her crisp and starchy aspect, from the white cap that crowned her lowered dark head, to the pragmatic lines about her mouth, down to the bleached apron covering her grey, floor-length dress. He frowned a little at the old-fashioned uniform, glancing from her to the antique-looking iron bed.

The nurse approached him, and with matronly authority that disregarded the inches of height he had over her, pulled his head down and placed her small hands on his forehead and behind his ears.

"Have I been in an accident?" he asked as she pushed back

his eyelids to examine his eyes. "Is this a hospital?"

She went on examining him, catching his hand to check his pulse. All readings were normal, and jotting down her notes, she finally glanced up at him, then nodded at a dark grey uniform, which lay folded over the bed's foot rail.

"What's this?" he asked, unfolding a pair of grey coveralls. "Wait. Where are my clothes and things?"

But by then the nurse had already left, closing the door behind her.

Outside his room, the hallway was lined with closed doors and dim yellow lights. He looked down one end of the corridor, and as he turned his head towards the other, his eye caught something pale disappearing just beyond the corner. It was but a glimpse, but it left him with the impression of splayed feet being dragged across the floor as if a body were being hauled away.

"Hello?" he called softly, uneasily, approaching the bend in the hallway, now noticing a glistening wet streak left behind where the feet had disappeared.

But around the corner, he found only a janitor mopping the floor, trailing glossy smears across the linoleum surface.

Greg turned back and started a little when he found the nurse standing close behind him, arms akimbo, regarding him with silent disapproval.

"Oh, there you are," he said with a sigh of relief. "I wanted to talk to—I—would you stop pulling my hand? I need to speak to the doctor."

She considered him for a moment, seeming puzzled by his resistance, then stepped back towards a square button on a nearby wall and poised her finger before it with a challenging look.

"Well, go ahead then," said Greg, thinking she was threatening to page the doctor.

She sniffed haughtily and pushed the button. For a few seconds nothing seemed to happen, and just when Greg began to wonder whether it was all a bluff, three orderlies in white uniforms came running from the other end of the hallway.

"Wait, wait a minute!" said Greg, raising his hands in a placating manner as he stepped back. "There's no need for this. I just want to speak with someone."

But the orderlies seemed deaf to him, continuing to reach out to grab him as he stepped back, until he broke out: "Alright, already! You've made your point. I'll get dressed. But after that, I need to speak to whoever's in charge."

This seemed to satisfy them, and they folded their arms and stepped back, allowing him to pass by and regain his room. They followed him and occupied the doorway, fixing him with mistrustful scrutiny. All three had their heads shaved and wore similar expressions of bored contempt, which gave the initial impression of them having the same build and height, especially when they showed up as a unit. But now Greg saw the largest of them had to duck his head through the door, while the other two just reached up to his shoulders.

He stared at them, waiting for all four—nurse included—to clear out.

They stared back, waiting for him to change into his uniform.

"Show's over," said Greg. "So, if everyone could just leave…"

They remained in place.

"You understand what I'm saying, right?" he asked, waving the grey coveralls at them dismissively.

But they remained rooted to their spots. He shrugged and sat on the edge of the bed with his arms folded.

"Or we could just sit here and have a stare-down."

Five minutes later they were still standing in the doorway, glaring at Greg while he rattled on about his favorite blood sport.

"So, it's the final round, and only two were left standing—each of them holding a knife—both looking equally gruesome, covered in all kinds of body fluids: sweat, saliva, snot—one of them was even bleeding. But the way those chefs chopped, sliced and diced vegetables, all while biting down on a ghost pepper was just—just—" his hands paddled the air as he struggled to find a succinct phrase to sum it up. "Ah, you just had to see it for yourself."

It was hard to tell from their invariable expressions whether or not they listened, or even understood him at all. Not that it mattered; he had hoped his prattle would annoy them into leaving, if not get someone's attention, preferably a doctor or a friendlier staff member with whom he could communicate.

To wake up to this without a word of explanation was one thing, but it was even more jarring to be expected to change in front of a crowd of strangers; had they treated him with decency, or at least said something to explain their cagey attitude, he wouldn't have minded as much. But he remained obstinate in the face of their persistent scrutiny, treating him like an inmate in a maximum security facility.

Struck suddenly with the thought, he glanced down at the uniform draped over his lap, checking for any label or emblem to identify the facility.

There was none, but he continued to stare at the coveralls, absorbed in thought, until, out of the corner of his eyes, he detected a shift in the orderlies' attitude as they unfolded their arms, and seemed about to step in and use force. Not wanting to give them that satisfaction, he stood up and, turning his back to them, wrapped the thin blanket around his waist like a towel before stepping into the coveralls. Then, dressed from the waist down, he removed both blanket and hospital gown, which gave rise to jeers from the orderlies, who chuckled and nudged each other over his rangy build.

Greg shrugged them off, pushing his arms through the sleeves, even as his face clouded with a mixture of anger and apprehension, and for the tenth time he wondered what the hell happened to land him in a place where, on the face of it, the nursing staff reigned unchecked, harassing patients and browbeating them into compliance.

But he felt somewhat less vulnerable now that he was dressed. And breathing away the dire notion, he turned to them with unruffled expression, still fastening the last Velcro strip.

"Alright," he said, smoothing down his sleeves for added effect, "I think I'm decent enough to speak to the head honcho here."

In response, they stepped back out and shut the door behind them with a click of the lock.

CHAPTER 2

Sometime later, Greg woke up to someone shaking him by the shoulders.

The room was dark save for the weak hallway light filtering through the open door, and the first thing he saw when he lifted his head was a glint of eyeglasses, worn by the man trying to rouse him from sleep.

"On your feet," said the stranger in a low voice, pulling him by the arm; but Greg, still in the confused state that comes from troubled sleep, remained tethered to the corner where he had slept for the past hour or so.

Earlier, he had protested his lockdown, first by calling through the door cracks, then by slamming himself against the door to exhaustion—or at one point, until the orderlies barged in with the implied threat of physical harm if he didn't stop. Again, he demanded to speak to someone; again they ignored him. He ran past them, making for the door, but was summarily caught and thrown back in.

Too battered to hurl himself against the door, he huddled in one corner, hoping to hide from view and ambush whomever delivered his meal. His tray was shoved in through a slot in the door. Nevertheless, he kept his post, ignoring the tray, which offered an unappetizing array of cold slops, purees, and a pile of wilted greens that smelled worse than it looked.

Time passed: the room darkened as the outside light began to fade. His eyes grew heavy, as did his head, which rested against his folded knees, and it was not long before he drifted off to sleep.

The stranger pulled Greg by the elbow and stood him up. He lurched a little from the sudden shift in position, his numb legs prickling with returning circulation. The stranger then slipped a black knit cap over his head, covering his eyes. Greg reached up to adjust it, but the stranger drew his hands away.

"Keep it on if you want to come with me," whispered the stranger.

"Where are we going?" asked Greg, resisting the stranger's towing hand.

"Hush. You'll get your answers soon. Now move."

Greg relented and allowed the stranger to lead him by the elbow as they walked through the silent corridors. At some point, they stopped before an elevator, and while they waited, Greg pretended to scratch his cheek, intending to push the edge of the cap higher up to sneak a peek. His guide caught on and slapped his hand away.

They disembarked on another floor, this one warmer than the previous. Some distance later, the stranger stopped to unlock a door, and in that brief moment, while he searched his keyring looking for the right one, Greg was able to uncover one eye and glance about. He glimpsed the stranger—a man in a suit who had his back turned to him—and saw little of the dim corridor before the click of the turning lock cued him to lower his hand.

The stranger ushered him through the door.

"Here we can speak without fear of disturbing others," he said, releasing his arm. "You may raise the cap enough for you to see, but keep it on your head."

Greg did so, looking around as he pushed back the cap. The fire from the wood-burning stove was the room's only source of light, deepening the red of the papered walls. Two armchairs faced the fire, and between them was a small table laid with a coffee set and a basket of pastries, which Greg eyed with languid interest. He averted his gaze to hide the hungry look, though hunger had sharpened his other senses, and whichever way he turned his head, he could not avoid the rich, sweet smell, suggestive of glaze and butter. More beguiling was the smoky scent of coffee, which the stranger began pouring into a porcelain eggshell cup, drawing out the act to amplify the thin gurgling sound. He stood tall in his brown suit and looked to be somewhere in his fifties, with receding reddish hair brushed back and a trimmed circle beard. His face crinkled in a benign smile as he turned to Greg.

"Please, sit down," he said, pushing the rimless glasses up his thin nose. "I'm told you haven't eaten anything since you woke up. It's still dark outside, but I like to have my breakfast early."

Greg lingered in the foyer, eyeing the room with suspicion, as though his first step into it would spring a trap. His roving gaze settled on a wall hung with framed diplomas.

"You a doctor?"

"Yes. I'm Dr. Carver."

"Good. How about you start by telling me why the hell am I here."

The doctor extended a saucer with a steaming cup to Greg, and when the latter did not move to accept it, set it down on the table by the empty chair.

"The truth is you were found outside our facility—unconscious—wearing a uniform much like the one you have on now."

"Outside," repeated Greg, steadying himself against the doorway until the floor behaved itself and stopped turning. Earlier, he could not remember much beyond the hike up a mountain trail. Now he had glimpses of bivouacking somewhere outdoors, but the memory had a hazy, dream-like quality to it, and he could not entirely settle whether his mind was recalling true events or using some archived memory to fill in the gaps.

"Outside where?" he asked. "What is this place?"

Dr. Carver smiled hospitably. "Please sit down. You look like you can barely stand."

Greg hesitated. It bothered him to go from being treated like a criminal to receiving an invitation to share a meal, and he had the inescapable feeling of being coaxed into something. At the same time, an audience with the doctor was what he had been after, and he told himself he would be a stubborn fool to refuse a meal he badly needed, as well as a chance to get some answers. He tentatively settled into the armchair and took his cup.

The first draft of the strong coffee surprised him into a

thoughtful pause, sending a pleasant rise of alertness up his brow that seem to converge between his eyes.

Carver, catching the candid expression, which softened his guest's guarded look, said: "Good, isn't it? I'm rather particular about coffee and always brew my own pot. I've been experimenting with different blends, but I think I rather like this one." He took a sip from his lifted cup, then sat back with a thoughtful expression. "The reason why I've called you here, my friend, is because we have a tricky situation. You don't belong here and neither should you stay. At the same time, I can't simply let you walk out."

Greg frowned at the cryptic remark. "Is this about my medical insurance?"

Carver answered him with an apologetic smile. "Perhaps I better start from the beginning. You see, this place is a joint mental health and correctional facility that implements the lifestyle of a monastery. Felons that are committed here must remain here until they're paroled. While they're here, they are made to live within reduced circumstances, subsisting on a simple yet nourishing diet—no drugs, alcohol, caffeine, sugar, or any other stimulants. The idea is to provide a secure and isolated community with little to distract them from long periods of contemplation—we even have them observe a vow of silence. Some might call it medieval, but carried out correctly, this lifestyle can yield results, and we've had successful cases to prove it. Of course, it's not all enforced silence: whenever they're ready or in need of counsel, we're here to offer them guidance—"

"Doctor," interrupted Greg.

"Yes?"

"What does that have to do with me?"

"Yes, yes—I'm coming to that," said Carver, bending forward to jab the fire with a poker and push back a log, sending a few sparks flying. "As I've mentioned before, we found you outside with nothing on you—no driver's license, no ID or anything apart from the standard issue uniform like the one you're wearing now. Not long before that, an inmate with a history of attempted escapes went missing, and when we found you, we'd assumed you were him. You were unconscious then—your face covered in dirt. But even after they cleaned you up, I wasn't aware that something was off. You see—" he concluded under the puzzled look manifesting on his guest—"you and he bear a remarkable resemblance to each other."

Greg leaned back a little, narrowing his eyes skeptically. "Can't be that remarkable…" he faltered out.

"Well, maybe his hair and beard were a little longer," Carver hastily qualified, "but otherwise, you could pass for his double: you look to be the same age, you both have the same shade of dark hair and eyes; that same strong face and aquiline nose; the same lean build, the same height—yes, the exact same height! You look skeptical but imagine my surprise. I had to measure you to be sure. It's incredible! On the records and to the staff, you and he are the same person. But I knew you weren't him when I saw you didn't have the same fresh scar he had. I performed an emergency appendectomy on him—and before you ask: no, it's not listed in his file. I haven't had the chance to amend that yet."

Greg continued to stare in bewildered silence, trying to settle whether or not he believed all this. The doctor, meanwhile, went on, peering over his glasses as he studied his subject.

"You know, it's funny: you two might have similar features, but you bear distinctly different miens—it's more apparent now that you're awake and animated—or perhaps I should say he's the one who's more animated: charming, quick to flash his white teeth in a disarming smile, or a good-natured laugh..."

"Sounds like a con artist," muttered Greg, getting out of his chair to pace the small perimeter of the room.

"While you," Carver continued, "you're tenser and more closed off than he is—you always have that vertical line between your eyebrows—yes, just like that! A frown line to his crow's feet! But then he's always—"

"Always smiling—yeah, I heard," interrupted Greg, growing impatient. "Look, you said it yourself: I'm not the man you're looking for. So why am I still here?"

Carver rubbed his chin with an awkward chuckle. "I don't have the authority to discharge a felon, or in this case, a person everyone believes him to be. Without anything to identify you, my hands are tied in that regard."

"What about that scar you mentioned...?"

"I told you I never had the chance to amend that."

"Fine. Fingerprints, then. I'm sure you keep a record of them in his file."

"Not with us, I'm afraid," said Carver, refreshing his cup of coffee. "I don't have access to his criminal file either. The local authorities might have a copy of it. I called them this morning to report his escape..."

"Call them again," said Greg, heading for the phone perched on the corner of the desk. "Tell them about the mix-up. If we can get a copy of his file—" He broke off, agitating the switch hook, trying to get a dial tone. All the while, Carver remained quiet, taking a few thoughtful sips of his coffee, until the younger man realized for himself the futility of using the phone.

"Yes, about that: it seems we have a problem with the phone lines in the area. It happened after last week's storm. We don't get any mobile coverage here either, and I had to get by using a pay phone at a nearby station. It's why I wasn't around when you woke up. I'll have to go back there again today to see if there's any news." He set down the cup and rose to face Greg. "Which brings me to my other point: I was hoping that while we try to track down our missing man, that you simply go on pretending you're him."

Greg still stood with the dumb receiver in his hand.

"Wh—How's that?" he stammered.

"I want to keep peace and order here," explained Carver. "The other inmates are not yet aware that one of them had managed to escape, and I'd rather it stays that way. They might try to do the same—or worse, start a riot…"

"A riot?" scoffed Greg. "When you have the place on lockdown and everyone's observing their vows of silence? Plus who's going to try anything when you've got hired thugs eager to tenderize any rowdy inmate?"

"Unfortunately, I can't enforce the lockdown for long. It's detrimental to the inmates' mental health, which is the last thing we want. Today we resume our routine, and I need you to be present amongst them. They observe their vows of silence, true, but they'll notice if an inmate is missing."

"And how long do you plan on keeping up the charade?"

"Until we find our man, of course."

"And if I refuse?"

"You're in no place to bargain," said Carver, setting down his cup. "On record and in the eyes of everyone, I still have my patient."

Greg considered him with growing unease. "You're not even going to report this, are you? Not until they find him and bring him back."

Carver gave a careless shrug. "Either way, I'm afraid you're stuck with us. But there's no reason why I can't make your stay here pleasant."

Satisfied with his answer, the doctor headed to a nearby sideboard, where a slab of pound cake waited for him along with ramekins of berries, jams and other spreads, leaving Greg to stare after him in confounded silence. But the latter soon realized he did not have to agree to any of this: it was still dark outside, and at this hour security would be lax. If he bolted for the door now…

"Yes, you could try to run," said Carver, his back turned as he sliced the cake, "but you'll get caught before even finding the nearest exit. Ever since our mutual friend found a way to slip through the cracks, we've blocked all possible exits and tightened security. Go ahead and try it if you like. I won't stop you…"

He hardly turned as he spoke, occupied with spooning berries and drizzling sauce judiciously over the slices of cake. Greg followed him with a sidelong gaze, unsettled by the feeling that the doctor read him like an open book; he could test his bluff, but then he was not eager to be thrown back into his cell anytime soon.

"You know I could sue you once I get out," countered Greg, knowing well the threat was about as effective as tossing a pebble at an invincible foe; but any attack, however futile, was preferable to admitting defeat.

Carver turned to face him, holding a plate of cake in each hand. "You think you've got a case? When I'm here doing my job detaining a man who, to all appearances, is the same inmate and lacks evidence to prove otherwise? Do you know how many inmates here claim innocence or say they're victims of a mix-up? You'd just be one of dozens who've said as much on any given day. You don't have a case, my friend. But if you insist on taking legal action, find yourself a good pro-bono lawyer, 'cause the others will drink your heart's blood before they're through with you."

Greg could only stare back with resentment and incredulity before his gaze drifted elsewhere. He was staring at the flames licking the stove's grille, trying to rally his scattered thoughts, when he noticed a plate of cake hovering at the edge of his vision, and turned to find Carver holding it up for him to take. Greg felt like lashing out; but the sight of the cake, glazed and garnished with berries, quelled any such reaction, not just because it looked incredibly edible—and he was famished at this point—but because he had more respect for food than to knock it to the ground. And in its current position, held up between him and Carver, the cake seemed a buffer against an angry outburst.

He broke into a helpless laugh. "First you lock me up, and now you're offering dessert. What next? Break my legs and give me a pedicure?"

Carver smiled, and a twinkle in his eyes seemed to suggest that he liked the idea, or at least found it amusing.

"You may think I'm being unreasonable, but I've said it before: I can make your stay with us pleasant. Even knowing what I know, I could have easily saved myself the trouble and left you locked up. We wouldn't be here having this conversation. But I still have my ethics, and I'd rather we work together: you play your part, and I'll make sure you're released the moment we find our runaway. Here's hoping we apprehend him before you've had a chance to get comfortable."

Greg tried to avoid glancing down at the offered cake, pursing his lips in a show of reluctance to stretch the silence a second or two longer. In reality, he was fresh out of ideas and had to own that, after all, it might be wiser to comply with the doctor for now, rather than antagonize him.

"God forbid I get too comfortable here," he murmured, accepting the cake.

"That reminds me," said Carver, heading for the desk. "There was one other thing that we found on you." He returned and placed a black, brick-like object on the table next to Greg's empty cup.

Something about the device's shape and size was familiar enough that Greg instantly swallowed the mouthful he was chewing. The hair at the back of his head bristled as he picked up the handheld cassette recorder, as if a ghostly touch had passed through him, leaving him cold and clammy.

"Where are we?" he asked, lifting his gaze with a lost expression, his voice croaky from the large bite he forced down.

Carver regarded him curiously. "I just told you, we're in—"

"No, I mean our location—this area..."

"Duncastor," answered the doctor. "Why?"

Greg said nothing, and instead opened the cassette recorder to look inside. "It's empty."

"Yes, I did find that odd..."

CHAPTER 3

Locked in his dark cell, Greg lay awake in bed, fidgeting with the compact black device, pressing the rewind and stop buttons to listen to the heavy click and spring-loaded clank that initiated and punctuated the faint whirring mechanics. He wanted to believe the coffee kept him up, but he knew too well it was the locked door that bothered him. Everything else was bearable in this situation—it was the locked door that kept bothering him. He could distract himself until, time and again, the fact that his door was locked fell like drops of cold water on his forehead. No other course of action presented itself to him just yet. All he could do now was wait and observe: he knew well enough no one was going to come looking for him—not while he was in between jobs, living in a four-door pickup truck, and had traveled to an undisclosed location without telling anyone about it.

Just two weeks ago, he had run into a former roommate, who

invited him for coffee at a nearby place.

"Must be nice living like Thoreau," the roommate had said at some point in their conversation regarding Greg's lifestyle.

Greg glanced up from stirring his coffee, then returned to his beverage with a chuckle: his friend—who came from a privileged background and tended to become starry-eyed whenever *Walden* was brought up—had either cherished an idealized notion regarding Greg's situation, or was fumbling to comment about it in a non-disparaging way.

"I'm just a poor team player who can't hold down a desk job," answered Greg, somewhat embarrassed by the comparison, which made him feel like his life was some elaborate performance put on to shadow one man's vision. He liked the autonomy of his life, getting by through a series of temporary jobs, the freedom and constant change it entailed, and the sense of self-reliance he gained even at the cost of financial security; but at his lowest, all his views turned on their heads, lost their golden radiance, and in the stark light he saw himself the way others no doubt did: a loser who couldn't hold down a long-term job, settle down, and sustain a normal adult life. There were lean days and dry spells when no work was available, and he weathered those periods by hanging out at the library or catching up on sleep. He learned to look out for those times, set aside cash—more to put gas in his car than food in his stomach, since he could always find some way to eat, but getting his car out of the tow yard cost more than he could afford. But when his needs were met, with enough money left over to see him through the lean times, he felt content, even proud of the small, independent life he made for himself.

When the bill came, which Greg insisted on splitting, he paid his share in a wrinkled bill and some loose change; and the roommate, after a furtive glance at his friend's emaciated wallet, awkwardly offered to "pull some strings" to help him find a job. It was meant in kindness, but it nonetheless nettled Greg, who surmised it was born of pity; he held back a sharp response, thanked his friend, and declined.

Besides, he was already taken with the idea of producing sound stories and documentaries for radio, if not for his own podcast. Not the most lucrative job, but that mattered little to him: the past weeks saw him working a myriad of temporary jobs through which he kept an audio diary of his insights and experience. But tiring of using himself as a subject, he moved on to interviewing his co-workers during lunch breaks or at the end of their workday. And while a few of them were leery or patronizing at first, a handful made use of having a captive audience receptive to their grievances, banter, and wild anecdotes. Not long after he began to hunt for subjects outside his immediate circle, and if some strangers opened up to him, it was because he was attentive and engaging—or greased their palms, whenever he could afford it.

It was then that he first heard of Duncastor and the abandoned building there that was rumored to be part of a black site—rumors that were circulated amongst truckers and drifters, some exaggerating the sinister aspect of the place, detailing with morbid relish the methods of enhanced interrogation that were being developed or deployed there, while others assumed the contrarian position and downplayed the horrors, if not downright dismissed the whole story as hyperbole. But, conjecture or not, after a string of personal and work-related stories, a change of subject was more than welcome to Greg, and the rumors were too good to ignore.

Greg stopped the rewinding mechanism when he detected rustling and soft thumps coming through the ceiling vent—or thought he did, since the quirky nature of unidentified noise is that it usually ceases whenever one stops to listen. Like a living body, no running building is without its small, unaccountable bumps and muffled clanks; yet even if they're mostly benign noise, at night they're magnified by the ever-present hush, and their unfamiliarity never fails to inflame the imagination of the sleepless newcomer.

Sometime later, when he opened his eyes to the same thumping noise, and half-rose to pay closer attention to it, he noticed thin phosphorescent lines cast by the slit windows and the eerie orange glow they gave as they heralded the rising sun.

He got out of bed and walked over to the sink, running a hand from chin to cheek and down again, rasping the grains of hair that had begun to sprout there.

The wall behind the sink showed a discolored patch, indicating a mirror had once hung there, while laid on the sink was a sealed packet containing a thumb toothbrush and tube of toothpaste the size of his little finger.

At least these are new, he thought, opening the packet; and while he brushed his teeth, he stared meditatively at the discolored patch on the wall.

Shortly thereafter, the orderlies unlocked his cell door and slid it open, and he lined up in the hallway with the other inmates for the headcount before they all filed in for breakfast.

Greg felt a measure lighter leaving behind the confines of his cell. The relief effaced the looming dread of returning to it, but all the same, he tried not to dwell on it and kept his gaze fixed ahead or on the floor as they shuffled into the dining hall, maintaining an outward appearance of sleepy obedience, while inwardly taking notes of his surroundings.

Even stripped to utilitarian minimalism, the hall retained some semblance of its former grandeur, illuminated by a slant of dusty sunlight from the lofty windows facing east, rendering radiant rectangles on the white floor which were bracketed by the two long tables in the shaded areas.

Men varying in size, age, and race all filed in with military-like discipline, each taking his assigned seat at the table. The sounds of chairs scraping back rose to the vaulted ceiling, as did a few stray coughs. But that was it. There was peace and order as soon as everyone took their seats.

How this order was achieved and kept was hard for Greg to see when no authoritative voice sounded to bark commands and rebuke nonconformity. His own seat was near the end of the table, allowing him to steal a cursory glance and estimate the number of heads: each table seated about five inmates on either side, he calculated, so there were about fifteen to twenty of them.

The orderlies wheeled in large pots on rolling tables, and from those they ladled oatmeal, odorous wilted greens, and a foamy broth into divided trays and served them with an enameled cup of water.

Greg looked down at his tray with a blank expression that betrayed little of his diminishing appetite. His peripheral vision told little of his neighbors' enthusiasm (or lack of) toward the served meal: everyone had to wait until everyone was served before they began eating.

He tried the broth, tolerated the oatmeal, and found the greens left a slimy aftertaste. And yet all around him inmates ate without complaint; some had even finished their meals before the others, retiring into an attitude of quiet contentment as they sat with their heads bowed and hands clasped on the table.

Next to Greg, a sanguine inmate soon finished his portion and gave a soft sigh of gratification as he ran his hand down his full belly in a manner less like a gourmand and more reminiscent of an expecting mother. The demonstrative gesture, though silent, somewhat stood out amid the funereal stillness, drawing Greg's curious attention, and his perplexed frown gave in to a half-amused smile as he glanced at his neighbor, as if to say: "That good, huh?"

The sanguine inmate merely smiled back with dumb enjoyment.

Something flew into Greg's eye. He started, dropping his spoon with a clatter that caused the nearby inmates to look up while his hand flew to the spattered eye, wiping away what he realized a moment later was a glob of oatmeal. With his good eye, he surveyed his immediate circle of inmates, most of whom returned blank stares while he knuckled the slop out of his eye.

Then he noticed the hard-bitten face of an inmate sitting opposite him, holding a spoon in the manner of a catapult that had just launched its missile. Though built like a retired prizefighter with cropped greying hair, child-like mischief shone in his pale eyes as he anticipated a reaction from his target, and the look of amused challenge was met with an uncertain glare from Greg.

Arbitrarily, the inmate sniffed and dropped his gaze to his tray, his thin eyebrows lifted and his lips pursed in a parody of dejection as he traced lazy circles in the shallow broth with his spoon.

Greg continued to stare after him, not sure what to make of the sudden shift—whether the inmate was trying to pick a fight or had acted on a whim and now lost interest. At length, he returned to his own tray, though now and then he cast wary glances at the inmate.

An uneventful minute or two passed, and having finished his oatmeal, Greg sat idly pushing the wilted greens around his tray, when a spoon was flicked at him, struck his face, and clattered on his tray.

The repeat offender made no effort of hiding his guilt as he observed Greg with a growing smile, dusting his hands to signify that he was done with his meal.

Greg, looking across the table at the inmate, leaned back and raised the enameled cup to take a sip of water before splashing the inmate with the rest of it. This wiped the smile off the inmate's face, who in turn imitated Greg, but chose to spit the mouthful of water that he took.

Greg retaliated by tossing his tray lengthwise like a frisbee at the inmate, who saw it coming and, together with his seated neighbors, ducked out of the way. Distracted for a moment by looking over his shoulder, the inmate this time did not see the enameled cup that Greg had next thrown at him until he turned and it struck his face. The blow did not hurt him as much as briefly blind him, allowing Greg to jump on the table and deliver a kick to his face.

The inmate's head snapped back, but he swiftly recovered, grabbing Greg's ankles and with a mighty tug fell him on the tabletop. He toppled his chair as he stood to his towering height and dragged Greg by the collar to the edge of the table, where he began to pummel him.

Once—twice the punches landed before Greg blocked the

third with a tray, gritting his teeth as he shoved the tray into the inmate's face.

The inmate stumbled back; and gaining his feet, Greg lunged at the inmate, clasping his arms about the thick waist, trying to no avail to upset his balance. They were locked in each other's grasp, each trying to throw the other onto the floor, when a slap of scalding liquid hit them both.

The inmate took the worst of it, having inadvertently shielded Greg; but even as steam rose from his soaked back, he neither flinched nor reacted, except to release his opponent.

"What part of maintaining peace and order here don't you understand?" said Dr. Carver, pushing back Greg's eyelids to examine his pupils.

"He started it," muttered Greg, glancing at the dividing curtain, behind which the inmate occupied the second bed. The two of them had been taken to the infirmary, where they sat draped in large blankets, waiting for dry coveralls to be fetched for them.

The doctor sighed as he lowered his glasses and tucked the penlight back into his coat pocket. "Consider this a fair warning: You might think—" Carver paused, glanced in the general direction of the second bed, then leaned in to whisper: "You might think you're not an inmate here, but we've agreed you're filling in for him, and therefore the same rules apply to you."

Greg turned away and sneezed, drawing the blanket closer over his shoulders. "Don't inmates here get any socks or sweaters or something?" he grimaced.

"I recommend bed rest to keep you warm and keep you out

of trouble," rejoined Carver, stepping back and towards the other bed, where he clicked his tongue in a chastising way, and then it was the inmate's turn to be examined.

Greg did not remember lying back and falling asleep, only a hazy awareness that he was swimming under the surface of consciousness; that his eyes were closed and yet he still saw the yellow ceiling light overhead eclipsed by an outline of a person standing over him.

He sat bolt upright, one hand already balled into a fist, but found no one had stood near him or was even in the room.

The curtain that separated the two beds was drawn back, showing a vacated bed and a small window open to a dense brush of spruce branches that almost poked their way through.

The next thing he knew he was being roused by the middle-aged nurse, who was shaking his half-covered shoulder. She jutted her chin to indicate the clean coveralls left for him on the side table.

Heavy-eyed, he smiled at her. "You know, if we keep seeing each other like this, people are gonna start talking."

In response, she pressed a finger to her lips, invoking the vow of silence.

Still, he was pleased to see that this time she left him and stood outside, granting him some privacy to dress.

As he sat up, Greg noticed his hand was still closed in a fist. He uncurled his fingers and found a small piece of paper folded in his hand. A glance over his shoulder reassured him that he was still out of the nurse's sight, and after sliding his legs into the coveralls, he unfolded the paper and found a simple drawing of a bed with an arrow pointing at the floor underneath it.

A minute later, the nurse returned to check on Greg, giving precursory hem for the intrusion before she briskly slid back the curtains and found his bed empty.

CHAPTER 4

It was a tight crawlspace. And after easing himself into it, lying flat on his stomach, and lifting his hand to close the sliding panel above, Greg realized that it was dark as well. He sighed dejectedly, wishing he had thought ahead and grabbed any spare penlight or emergency torch he might have found at hand before going through the trap door under the bed.

Overhead from the infirmary came the muffled clink of drapes being sharply drawn by the nurse, and it was enough to start him crawling into the denser dark of the dusty passageway. The question was whether or not Carver knew about this crawlspace, where it led to, and whether he'd be waiting for him at the other end.

But the possibility did not slow Greg down, even as he struggled to slink through the crawlspace. It was about as wide as his shoulders and, tucking his elbows close, he progressed with a series of small motions that began with him placing one arm in front of the other to drag himself forward while simultaneously lifting his hips to push with his toes.

However, not long after, his shoulders began to scrape harder against the walls of the crawlspace, reminding him how easily he could wedge himself into a tight spot, and his mind ran a number of morbid scenarios, from getting trapped at dead ends with no chance of turning back, to stumbling across colonies of inquisitive roaches, to being shadowed by bold and hungry rats.

Well, you haven't found any bones, and nothing brushed against your hands or feet for you to start raising red flags, was the thought with which he spurred himself, if spurring was possible in a confined space. The absence of insects was reassuring, and the dry warmth that radiated from the walls was not unpleasant. Still, he could almost swear the walls constricted just now. It was impossible to tell in the dark, but he felt a distinct sense of compression pressing against his back, arms, and chest that made him hope it was more latent claustrophobia setting in, rather than the walls actually closing in.

He hit a corner in the passageway when his hand met with a wall in front of him, then detected a slight draft coming from his left, and groped the empty space there to determine that the path continued in that direction.

It was something of a struggle making that tight turn—negotiating his body into contorted positions, holding and releasing his breath while he rotated himself into lying on his side to be able to move along the corner's bend.

Having made that turn, he now noticed light shining some feet away. Or rather, it was a small lightbulb that glowed quietly, not enough to illuminate this branch of the tunnel. And yet somehow, the closer he got to it, the brighter it seemed to shine.

It gave off a silvery halo now that it was almost within reach—or would be as soon as Greg closed the few inches of distance between them and stretched his arm to it. Instead, he lowered his head to cough when a wave of stench hit him: not the reek of sewage or decaying carcasses; there was a living quality to this smell that he couldn't quite put his finger on—didn't want to put his finger on. And the light that a moment ago seemed only inches away had moved four or five feet back, glowing and dimming with rhythmic intention.

He narrowed his eyes, straining to make out what it was, whether some form of a bioluminescent insect, or an appendage attached to some larger creature, like an anglerfish luring its unsuspecting prey.

But just as he was about to laugh off the notion (after all, how far was he from the deep sea?) the glowing thing slithered away with frantic speed, and he could not help the gasp of surprise that, a second later, repeated itself—not echoed by the walls, but mimicked by what waited beyond, where the glowing thing had disappeared.

Whatever it was, it caught the sound of his gasp and now mimicked again in its shrill, eldritch voice, sending wafts of the stench that he smelled before: something like moist dirt and raw eggs.

Greg scrabbled back, not noticing in his panic how the floor seemed to give under him.

Something moved in front of him, lashing the space he occupied a second ago. He heard it scrape the floor and walls, searching for him while he pushed back to avoid it, struggling to retreat farther back in this confined space; that is, until he felt something thin and delicate brush against his cheek.

Whether tongue or antenna, it served to locate him. And having found him, the thing struck closer and would have caught Greg had he not scrabbled back, scraping his hands and elbows in his effort, until his feet stopped against the corner that he had struggled to pass through earlier. Worse yet, the creature had effortlessly closed the distance and was now about a foot away, sweeping along the tunnel walls, intent on finding him, while all he could do was lie prone, pressing his body to the floor, his only shelter then, as if hoping he could sink into it. His head lay sideways, buried in the crook of his arm to dampen any sound he might make and keep his trembling breath from stirring the air.

It was then he noticed the floor was starting to buckle under him. Alarmed at this, he tried to shift his weight, when something spongy and wet caught his raised arm, coiling around the wrist before giving it a violent jerk.

Greg pulled back, bending his arm at the elbow to resist the winch-like force that began to reel him in.

All of a sudden, the floor beneath him collapsed. His legs swung in the air while he held on to the ledge, but it too crumbled under his weight and he fell below.

Carver stood at the foot of the infirmary's empty bed.

"He was last seen here?" he asked.

The nurse nodded.

The doctor nodded as well, more to himself, pushing a tongue in his cheek, as if puzzling over a tricky situation, though when he spoke next, it was with certainty.

"Call them back. He's still in the building."

The nurse left to do his bidding without so much as a look of doubt at the man whose word was law in this establishment.

"Perhaps the west wing..." he said, almost as an afterthought.

Greg lay sprawled amongst the debris and over a pile of old, thin mattresses that broke his fall. He rolled over to one side, coughing up the dust he had inhaled. Bits of the ceiling broke off, showering him with more plaster dust and debris, and he winced and crossed his arms protectively over his head.

Then, squinting up at the ceiling and the ragged hole that yawned over him, he stumbled to his feet, and looked back at the hole expectantly. Nothing came through it, however, and after a few seconds had passed, he began to wonder whether he had really encountered something back there, or whether it was something dreamt up by his cracked skull—and for that matter, which was worse than the other?

He recalled the tendril-like touch grazing his cheek, and with a slight sneer of revulsion scrubbed that spot with his hand, as though to wipe away any trace left there, phantom or otherwise.

The room he found himself in was large and dingy: its only source of light came from a large bay window, securely barred with diamond grilles, through which shone the pale, solemn radiance of an overcast sky, holding the shadows at bay. Though it might have once served as a sun room, it now housed shelving units loaded with boxes, as well as castoffs like the old and stained mattresses that were piled up in one corner.

Whatever use it had, the room was kept locked, as Greg found to his dismay when he tried the handle of the metal door.

He lifted an uneasy gaze back up to the hole in the ceiling, which seemed his only exit at the moment, and which he reckoned he could reach if he moved some of the boxes and shelving units to form rudimentary stairs; it was preferable to remaining locked in, and yet he was not ready to climb back into it just then.

Without much thought, he pulled out one of the cardboard boxes and found it heavier than he had estimated. Others were likewise heavy, filled with stacks of papers—some stapled, some loose, some gathered in folders—and Greg began rifling through them, searching for anything that might help: layouts or blueprints of the building that could guide him; reports or records of inmates; even delivery invoices to see if and when supply or laundry trucks made it all the way up here…

At first, he stole nervous glances at the hole every few minutes whenever he thought he heard something, or caught a glimpse of a shadow darting just out of his range of vision. But presently he sat cross-legged on the floor with his back to the window, skimming through documents under the wan light and dividing them into stacks according to their recorded date. The task demanded the same level of focus required to piece together an intricate jigsaw puzzle—especially when he had to stop and consider undated scraps and notes, studying the penmanship, content and type of paper before placing them in one pile or other.

The gist of his fragmented findings—the various letters, deeds, documents, and invoices—told the following: starting from the early 1900s, the house had either been inherited or sold, repaired and prepared for occupation, then abandoned once the repair project fell into hiatus, and left to fall into disrepair. This cycle of the estate's planned renovation and fall into neglect repeated itself over the decades, though none of the letters explained why everything came to a grinding halt every time the repair work was almost finished. One note hinted that the money simply ran out at some point, while another letter evasively said, "the men refuse to work under these conditions."

He was in the process of pulling another box off the shelf when he heard something fall to the floor with a clatter. Whatever it was, it fell in a shadowy patch between the wall and the shelving unit, and Greg had to reach his hand behind the shelves till his fingers touched something plastic. He clawed at it, sliding it towards him, and pulled out a cassette tape, unmarked and unlabeled but coated with dust, which Greg mechanically blew off, wondering whether it belonged to the runaway inmate. He had no intention of going back to his cell just to retrieve the handheld recorder and listen to it, but he wanted to keep the tape on the off chance it contained something of interest. The coveralls had no pockets for him to stash his find, so instead he tucked it into one sleeve as he rolled it up, securing the cassette tape in the broad folds.

None of the boxes he looked through afterwards yielded anything useful: a lot of them held old issues of newspapers and magazines, indecipherable research reports, and papers that were either too damaged or seemed irrelevant to his search.

The strain of reading faded text under a fading light was starting to wear on his eyes, and not having slept much the night before, Greg soon he found himself beginning to nod off. He did not remember carrying a sheaf of papers with him as he shuffled towards the mound of old mattresses, or why he had them in hand; all he registered then was the comfort of a spongy surface that relieved his back and feet, and for which he expressed a grateful sigh before drifting off.

Each time he surfaced to reality—just conscious enough to glimpse the dim room, perceive that he inexplicably held papers close to his chest, or close his mouth, which heavy sleep had slackened—oblivion would part under him like the broken page of water and swallow him whole.

His eyes were closed, but his mind's eye was open to the room, its gaze fixed on the hole in the ceiling, whence something emerged, softly creeping as it carried its black mass down the walls, extended its neck toward him, and soundlessly stretched open its maw behind his head like a darkened doorway while he lay paralyzed by sleep.

In an instant something large caught him, and like a python's coil, it closed around him from the waist up and held him fast. His legs gave a startled twitch before he felt a sharp jab to his side. Soon he stopped struggling as his muscles relaxed, his limbs went slack, and his mind dissolved into a vacant stupor.

CHAPTER 5

His head felt heavy and full of lead, and the rest of him felt creaky and loathsome—so loathsome that sleep seemed to have washed its hands of Greg, remaining unbidden even as he stubbornly kept his eyes closed. He restlessly turned on his bed, trying sides and positions that would ease his stiff back.

Small, incidental noise reported nearby: a small creak of hinges followed by the crackle of burning kindling; a bubbling of liquid being poured into a cup or bowl, and the polite clinks of porcelain and tableware.

Even with his eyes closed, Greg was able to follow what was happening just by listening. And not having heard the sound of approaching footsteps, he started when a cool hand pressed against his forehead and cheek.

"I can see that you can't sleep," said Dr. Carver, drawing back Greg's eyelids to examine his eyes. "Don't fight it and try to sit up. Slowly, now. Good—lie back down if you start to feel lightheaded. How do you feel?"

“Hungry,” was Greg’s plain, hoarse reply that had a note of bafflement, as if the answer surprised him.

Dr. Carver smiled at his patient’s expression of appetite. “I have the soup ready, but I have a feeling crackers would go well with it. I’ll be right back.”

He slipped back into the room’s dark corner, beyond the small radius of light offered by the wood stove, and vanished. The room had the same appearance as the office where Greg had sat with Carver (was it yesterday?) yet seemed larger, with a stately four-post bed on which he lay, oddly placed in the middle of the room, next to the wood stove and table that carried the covered pot and dinnerware.

Last thing he remembered was the locked room with all the boxes and papers, the sleep he fell into, and the needle-like jab in his right side that followed. The jab itself was unaccountable at first, until he surmised the orderlies must have found him after he had fallen asleep and sedated him. It made little sense given he was already unconscious, outnumbered, and not in any state that would warrant a sedative. And yet, as he lifted the hospital’s green gown to examine the site of the needle jab, he saw that his body had reacted to it, leaving a swollen, angry mark just above his hip that was tender to the touch.

He had it in mind to ask Carver about it, but the doctor was taking his time for someone fetching a glass of water and… what else did he say he was fetching?

The boy opened the closet door, turned on the light, and found his brother curled up, asleep on the floor.

"Ory," he said, stooping down to shake his twin's shoulder. "Ory, wake up. I got food."

If the lights had hardly disturbed the dozing twin, the mention of food jolted him awake.

"What'd you get?" asked Ory in a voice raspy with sleep as he snatched the bag from his brother's hand and began to wolf down what he thought was a plain sugar donut until he registered the tart taste.

"Jelly?" he asked, his small face pinched with distaste.

"Sorry, it was meant for me."

"Why'd you give it to me, then?"

"It's okay, I already ate one," the boy shrugged, still regarding the donut in Ory's hand with interest.

Greg opened his eyes. Gone was the glow of the wood stove, replaced by the weak predawn light coming in from the window to his left.

He was back in the infirmary and back in his grey coveralls, now ripe with dried sweat.

Two symptoms manifested themselves just then: first was the ache from his right side near the kidney; then, as his lips curled in a grimace, Greg felt the delicate cracking of a thin layer of something that had congealed over his lips. He touched his upper lip, and in the blue gloom saw flecks of blood on his fingertips.

"Doctor?" he called out to the empty room, looking around as he got out of bed, half-expecting Dr. Carver or even the nurse to show up in answer.

But as soon as his feet hit the cold linoleum floor, Greg heard a series of explosive bursts going off in the hallway. They sounded like gunshots, though somehow the idea seemed absurd in a place like this. All the same, he held his breath and inched his head from behind the door frame to peek outside.

The hallway was barely lit by a number of sconces casting feeble cones of yellowish light, but there was no mistaking the bodies of the orderlies that lay on the floor.

Farther ahead, a large man in coveralls limped towards the elevator that chimed to announce its arrival. The double doors slid open, washing the hallway floor with a long streak of light that was blotted by the man's tall shadow as he stood a moment in front of the elevator before stepping in and letting the doors close behind him.

Greg stepped into the hallway, casting wary glances at the bodies as he passed them by: one slumped against the wall, another had fallen to his side, and a third sprawled facedown.

He reached the elevator, pressed the call button, then pressed it again, wondering why it did not light up in response. Then he noticed the card reader slot, and glanced back at the orderlies, thinking one of them should have a key card on him.

As the one who lay facedown was the closest, Greg tried him first, and began to roll him over to reach for the front pocket when he heard a wet sound and glimpsed blood or something like it spurt out. But it was the fetid smell of offal mixed with a fecal stench that surprised him into nausea and sent him staggering back to vomit the contents of an empty stomach.

Cold water spluttered from the infirmary's sink. Greg rinsed the acrid taste of bile out of his mouth before splashing his face. Patches of the coverall's fabric that had soaked blood from the floor adhered to his knees and shins. An after-sick giddiness washed over him, and he gripped the edges of the sink to steady himself. His head burned beneath the water-cooled skin, and his hollow-eyed face, sitting between hunched shoulders, stared back at him from the mirror above the sink as he tried to rearrange his thoughts.

As far as he knew, there was a shooter on the loose—an inmate from the looks of it, though God knows where he got the gun from—and judging by the deserted halls, everyone had gone into hiding, leaving him alone to fend for himself. It didn't matter, as long as the shooter didn't decide to double back here. All the same, this was his chance to escape, and he better stop wasting his time trying to work the elevator when the stairs would do just as well.

Greg started again for the hallway, stepping over the bodies and lifting the coverall's collar to cover his nose against the stench. He stopped mid-stride when he remembered the broken glass covering the grounds outside; and looking around, he settled on the orderly slumped against the wall, and crouched before him with a perfunctory murmur of apology as he began taking off his shoes.

"What are you doing?" he heard spoken to him, and whipped his head around to look over his shoulder.

No one stood behind him. Yet the voice had been close enough for him to instinctively cover his ear against the tickling breath.

"What are you doing?" he heard again.

This time the voice came from ahead—rather from the orderly, who had been blankly staring down, but now fixed Greg with an accusatory glare.

Greg dropped the orderly's foot, staring wide-eyed as he

clambered back from the body.

He had taken it for granted that the orderlies were dead and gone; and yet now, from where they sat or lay motionless—neither breathing nor wincing—their eyes followed him as he managed to find his feet and bolted down the other end of the hallway—away from the elevator; away from their terrible gaze.

CHAPTER 6

"—I—uh——I just…

"I'm having trouble s-speaking right now. I just need a moment—to get my bearings. I'm recording this on a tape—some tape I found. A blank cassette tape, as far as I know. I can't remember where. No, wait, it was in that room—but never mind. Anyhow, my name is Greg. And I just want—I just need to record myself talking. It helps. Maybe it will serve some other purpose later, like evidence or something. But right now, I just need it to feel calm. And normal. I don't know why I'm out of breath when I stopped running ages ago. Let me just catch my breath. I need to focus. The time now is... never mind, I can't seem to find any clocks or anything. But judging from the narrow window, the sun is coming up now… Anyway, I just witnessed—no, scratch that—I didn't witness anything. I only saw the aftermath of a shooting. I woke up in the infirmary, heard some shots, went into the hallway and found three orderlies on the floor. There was a man—

an inmate—leaving the scene. I only saw him from the back just as he stepped into an elevator, but I'm almost sure he was wearing the same grey uniform as the other inmates. Then the doors closed and that was all I saw of him. The only victims I saw were orderlies. I think they're dead but… I couldn't tell. The hallway was kind of dark, and I thought—I mean, I didn't check, but I was almost sure they were—I mean, I thought I saw—

"Anyway, I guess I must have blanked out or something, because the next thing I knew I found myself in the corridor just outside our cells. I didn't expect they'd be on the same floor, but anyway—right now, they're all empty. The entire floor is empty if you don't count me and the—um, the victims. I don't know if there was a mass prison break or everyone just went into hiding. Anyhow, I mentioned an elevator and I'm going back there now to—

"Wait. Did I take a wrong turn? No, this is the right place… the elevator's there. But the bodies—they're not here. This can't be right: the hallway is empty—clean, even. The floor's all damp like someone's just mopped it. But the walls are still stained. And there's also that weird smell… it's not disinfectant. It's not ammonia either. I know that smell, but…

"Just what the hell happened here?"

"Greg here again. I've found a staircase and I'm going down. Screw it. Screw this entire place. I'm not stopping on any floor till I reach the ground level. I think this is it. Let's see—

"Alright, this looks like the lobby—there's the front desk, and—yes, there's the glass double doors of the main entrance. Are they locked? Of course they're locked. Sturdy locks and thick glass. There has to be a fire extinguisher somewhere around here I could use. I'll keep you posted."

The handheld recorder sat idle on the front desk while Greg rifled through the drawers for keys, money or any such useful items. At first, he found nothing more than office supplies and stationery, but a junk drawer yielded a penlight and a large pair of sewing scissors, which Greg appraised before setting them aside next to the recorder.

In the distance, something resonated at intervals from the corridors connected to the lobby; spectral noise, the tail end of echoes that seemed to come from within the bowels of those corridors. At times they sounded deceptively loud and close, enough to cause Greg to lift his head and look over the front desk, expecting to see someone or something emerging from the corridors. Thinking perhaps the lobby was not as deserted as it seemed, he first lobbed a paperweight then a box of staples from behind the desk, each time ducking to see if the noise attracted anyone or anything that might be lurking out of sight. No one showed up, and though nothing came of it, the sensation of not being alone remained ever-present.

The desk drawer cabinets had little else to offer, or so it seemed at first. On a hunch, Greg tried them again, this time searching more thoroughly, until his fingers brushed against a thick piece of paper taped to the underside of the main drawer. The paper turned out to be an envelope, which held a single key inside.

"When it rains, it pours," he murmured a few moments later through a half-smile to the handheld recorder as he crossed the lobby towards the front door. "Here's hoping that my luck has taken a turn for the better."

There was still the issue regarding footwear, but first Greg wanted to make sure the key did indeed unlock the glass doors. He stood before them now, in a patch of light that slanted through the glass and painted a broad band of radiance on the floor, making it blessedly warm underfoot.

And yet, there was an abrupt shift in the atmosphere as soon as he stepped into that island of light. The mysterious echoes stopped, as did some perpetual ambient hum that droned unnoticeably in the background, so that its presence was only marked by its absence.

Greg, key in hand poised before the lock, looked about with uncertainty, unsettled by the abrupt, vacuum-like silence.

Then came a low wispy sound, halfway between a whir and a high-pitched whistle, before his head snapped back, as if he had been punched in the face.

A stab of pain speared through his sinuses and up his forehead. The recorder, scissors, and key he carried all clattered on the floor as his hands flew to cover his nose.

He recovered shortly and, blinking away the tears, lowered his hands to find his palms smeared with blood.

Another stab of pain came on, this time radiating from his right side to his lower back with a burning severity that left him with no strength to stand on his legs. He fell to his knees, doubling over until his forehead nearly touched the floor. Perspiration soaked his back; cold air that silently whistled in through his set teeth was forced out in weak, ragged groans. His arms were crossed beneath his chest—the right hand a white fist, the left a petrified claw at his lower right flank.

Sunlight hurt his eyes, now gaining the intensity of a spotlight trained on him.

A caustic grin flashed through his grimace: *Keep it together!*

Whatever it is it can wait until we're out and far off!

For all that, he could not bring himself to raise his head, let alone move. And what felt like a spray of glass splinters lacerating his insides made him wonder how he would make the long trek down the mountain.

Time and again he came close to calling out for someone, only to bite it back.

Not now, not here, he growled inwardly, addressing his body in a bargain. *I'll get help outside. Please...*

Just then, a pair of feet emerged from the dark and stood to Greg's left, almost toeing the shadow cast by his semi-prostrate form.

Greg noticed the feet, blanched by the sun, and slowly rotated his head, turning his eyes up at the stranger. From his position, he could see little past the grey-clad ankles of the stranger, whose figure seemed to tower and melt into the shadows; moreover, a swarm of spectral diamonds of every bright color winked and flickered brilliantly in the air between him and the stranger.

"Please—please—" he breathed shakily, not sure what he was pleading for.

The stranger raised his arm until the slope of light that fell on Greg was pierced by the barrel of the gun leveled at his head.

But on his part, Greg was blind to the stranger's intentions: his gaze had dropped to the floor, staring blankly and dreamily down, listening to an odd and distant whistle. The pain had somewhat ebbed, but he was still afraid to get up lest the slightest movement would again trigger it.

The stranger must have said something, though his voice

had a muffled quality to it and was moreover overwhelmed by the incessant whistle. He crouched down and repeated the cryptic sentence, his voice closer but all the same slow, thick and viscous.

All the while, Greg kept his gaze downcast, fixated on the lazy swirl of the shimmering dust and the porous texture of the stained grey fabric that stretched over his left thigh. His awareness was dissolving, effervescing into fragments, lost in all the fine details that now overwhelmed his senses; he remained open-eyed yet unresponsive, his mind unable to register the muzzle pressed against his left temple.

CHAPTER 7

Clark ducked into the room and all but closed the door behind him. He was one of four inmates who took advantage of the chaos that ensued from the shooting incident and managed to slip away while the orderlies were distracted with gathering everyone to herd them to a safer area.

The main entrance was locked, and the stray inmates had to fall back to finding another way out. But while the orderlies were gone, and their living quarters were for the time untenanted, Clark and his friend, Nader, ransacked their rooms, chiefly searching for keys, but also taking what they could find: money, clothes, and anything they could use in their escape. This was left to Nader, who turned drawers and cabinets inside out while Clark kept a lookout for any threats.

"What is it?" Nader asked, emerging from under the bed when he heard Clark come in.

"I think they got someone," whispered Clark, peering through the crack in the door.

"What?"

Clark turned to Nader. "I said I think they got someone," he said, then turned back to look out.

"One of us?"

"Can't tell," answered Clark, sticking his blond head outside the door for a better look. "Well, it's a big guy—"

"What?"

"I said it's a big guy," hissed Clark over his shoulder, "and he's carrying someone; not an orderly, though."

"The guy carrying or the guy being carried?"

"Both," said Clark, then corrected himself: "I mean neither of them are in white."

"You don't think it's the shooter, do you?"

"I don't know..."

"What?"

Clark, growing tired of looking over his shoulder to answer every question, huffed impatiently. "If he is the shooter, I'll happily kiss his hairy, homicidal hands, alright? Now shut up and keep looking."

"Wake up," mumbled the boy, nudging his brother. "It's your turn to go out today."

"Yeah," sighed the brother, opening his eyes to the darkness of their narrow quarters as he sat up.

The boy tried to go back to sleep, but noticed his brother stalling.

"What's wrong?"

"I don't know," answered the brother. "I have a bad feeling, but I don't know why."

The boy squinted sleepily as he sat up. "I finished my homework this time. Ms. Bower won't have anything to be mad about." His brother remained quiet, so the boy went on: "I took care of Dave yesterday. He won't bother you. If he tries anything, tell me and I'll make him eat dirt tomorrow."

"No school tomorrow, remember?" said the brother, still sounding morose. No amount of reassurance seemed to lift the weird sense of dread that overcame him. He was deaf to the boy's exasperated sigh, and hardly registered the gentle head-bump the boy gave him by way of a reassuring forehead touch.

"Hey," said the boy, and waited for his brother to turn his head to look at him. The brother, expecting words of reassurance, heard: "Donut forget the donuts today," before his snickering twin dove back into the heap of blankets.

"I'll bring back those gross custard-filled ones," grumbled the brother.

"I'd still eat them," answered the boy willfully. "I'd eat an entire box."

"I bet," rejoined the brother. "If you could eat jelly donuts, you'll eat anything, I bet. I bet if you went to see the doctor, he'd say you've got a serious case of sewer mouth—"

"Shut up, Ory," said the boy, kicking his brother's back.

"Ha! You're Ory now, remember? Today's my turn to be—"

Greg lay asleep in a bathtub half-filled with water that by now merely retained the memory of heat. The tub was deep enough to cradle him with his head resting on the sloped end, but not long enough to accommodate his whole body without having to bend his legs at the knees. His arms, loosely folded over his middle, were submerged under the cloudy water that tried to throw back the filtered sunlight in its languid, breeze-stirred motion, gently lapping at Greg's chest, knees, and the white inner walls of the tub.

The drenched coveralls he wore invited a chill that roused him. His neck issued a series of muffled cracks as he began to move, first looking through his lashes at the white and silver blur that accounted for the bathtub's rim and its fixtures, then surveying the tile and plaster walls that closed around him, before finally lifting his vacant eyes to the small latticed window perched up in a corner near the high ceiling, open to a fair day and now favoring the dank and narrow bathroom with splintered shafts of light.

He felt a twinge behind his eyes and closed them in a weary frown, wondering where he was and how he ended up here. His last memories before he blacked out were hazy images of the lobby, the key from the envelope, and the affliction that caused him to double up before the glass doors. Some residual pain still lingered, though it was but a ghostly impression at this point; moreover, a fresh memory diverted his attention just then, though he could not settle whether the flashback came from a real event or a vivid dream.

In it, he was in the selfsame room and position, reclining half-asleep in the tub, when a stranger appeared, took him by the shoulders, and shoved him underwater to—

No, that wasn't it: the tub may be half-filled now, but it had been dry then.

The stranger had clamped his hands over Greg's face to

smother him, provoking the latter to thrash and kick, lashing the stained water into a froth—(but wasn't the tub dry then?) before a splatter of red liquid shot from his mouth, trickling over the stranger's hands as he tried to—tried to…

Greg absentmindedly rubbed his forehead, trying to get a firm grasp on the loose fragments of that episode. His gaze drifted over the greasy but otherwise white tub and the bare plaster walls, both innocent of any red stains. The water was murky, true, but that might be due to the blood his coveralls had soaked up from that terrible scene in the hallway.

It was probably a dream then. Or else he had suffered a seizure, was held down by one of the orderlies, and in the throes of a fit had bitten his own tongue; it accounted for the stranger holding him down and the blood spurting from his mouth, but not why he was left soaking in the tub. Moreover, his tongue felt fine as he gingerly pressed it against his teeth, showing not the least sign of injury, though it did register an odd taste.

Nothing added up. He breathed out in frustration and gave an involuntary shudder against a sudden draft that stoked the cold.

Behind him came a sharp click, towards which he turned his head, straining to look over the tub's high wall. He tried to raise himself, but found his body weak and heavy, so that by the time he managed to grab either side of the tub to hoist himself up—fell back when his hands slipped on the slimy rim; tried again and managed to raise himself to his knees—by then the bathroom door had swung shut, leaving Greg to stare half-stupefied at the closed door.

"Well, that could have gone better," came a male voice faintly through the bathroom door. "Things went south the moment they brought you back."

"Who are you?" demanded Greg, still kneeling in the tub, hands clutching either side to hold himself up with water dripping down the sleeves.

"As always, I went off half-cocked and tried to take matters into my hands," the voice went on, talking over Greg's question, "But I had no choice—"

"Quit hiding and come talk to me straight!" called out Greg, assuming a gruff tone to hide the slight tremble in his voice. He was confused, cold, and fresh out of patience.

But even if his call overwhelmed the man's voice for a moment, it droned on: "Anyway, I thought I'd scare them off to clear the way. It went about as well as you might imagine..."

This time Greg managed to climb out of the tub without incident, waterlogged coveralls clinging to him and streaming water on the floor as he steadied himself against the wall and took a few coltish steps towards the door.

He stood to one side of the door, his forehead and nose almost pressed against the frame as he stealthily curled his fingers around the door knob, listening to the man on the other side ramble on unawares. His intention was to swing the door open and catch him off guard. But as he listened, he began to discern a compressed quality of the voice, as if it came from a device. He opened the door a crack and peeked through to find his handheld recorder sitting on a wooden chair by the door, playing a message recorded on tape.

"Do what you have to do, and come find me later. But don't take your sweet time, or you might as well use those knives against yourself."

The day room was bright and quiet. In it, inmates sat or sprawled on whichever patch of furniture or ground they could claim that offered the most comfort and exposure to sunlight. Most were colossally large but harmless and content, so long as they were warm, rested, and well-fed.

Dr. Carver sat at a temporary desk, his pen scratching the quiet as he updated some of the reports. A nurse sat on a chair amongst the heavy-lidded inmates, mending one thing or another, legs crossed at the ankles, her workbasket at her feet. Now and then, an inmate would stand up and shuffle towards another spot in the room, prompting the nurse and Carver to look up from their respective work and study the drifting inmate's attitude to read his intent; but if the inmate's sleeve happened to have an orange armband, they returned to their work, knowing well he wanted nothing more than to find a warmer spot.

Usually the day room only received a certain portion of the resident inmates; now most of the population crowded the small space, save for a handful of inmates who went missing, and two more who tried to stir up trouble and were now restrained in another room.

Dog-eared paperbacks, decks of cards, and tattered magazines were handed out, which Carver had allowed on this occasion to mollify the inmates while the orderlies were away, hunting down their missing brethren.

Carver sighed and turned his attention to a small brown bottle sitting on his desk, catching the sunlight and casting an illuminated amber shadow on the surface of the desk. He tipped the bottle back and watched the translucent red capsules glow sympathetically within their vessel.

Several inmates looked up from their cards and books as two of the orderlies returned, herding in an inmate whose hands were cuffed behind his back. Upon their arrival, Carver's face eased into a smile of relief, and he beckoned them to approach his desk.

The orderlies, Toby and Roman, sat the inmate down, and stepped back, flanking him from either side.

"Holden!" Carver had all but cried out. "So good of you to join us. I was hoping we could talk."

He nodded at Toby and Roman to release the inmate's hands.

Holden, bear-like and middle-aged, a cavalier smile implicit in his pale eyes, sat still, save for the minor tugs caused by the orderlies undoing the plastic cuffs.

"You know we are still observing our vows of silence," said Carver, turning his attention back to the medicine bottle, "and I believe it is crucial to maintain such vows, even in these dire circumstances. Peace and order should be maintained for everyone's well-being. That is the heart of our program. It's not easy, I'll grant you that—not even for us who have to make sure they're not only observed but are also maintained in spirit.

"I have been vigilant in my efforts—" Carver droned on, while Holden sat back, resting his forearms on his thighs, letting his hands hang between his knees. The spark of mischief that had lit his eyes a minute ago was gone as he surveyed the room. He could recite from memory Carver's oft-repeated prattle on the virtues of his program, and knew well that Toby and Roman were about as bored as he was: out of the corner of his eyes he could see how Roman balanced himself on the balls of his feet, while Toby vigorously tilted his head from side to side to release a kink in his neck, both wired with nervous energy, anticipating the end of Dr. Carver's speech so they could drag Holden away for some *disciplinary actions*. The euphemism was Carver's, but the orderlies couldn't care less what he called it as long as they got to dispense it.

"As you can see," said Carver, sweeping the room with his gaze, "our program has brought on the benefits of a lobotomy without its detriments..."

He stopped then, interrupting himself in the middle of his speech that even Holden turned to look at him. Across the desk Carver extended his hands with the palms up, inviting Holden to extend his own large paws. Holden kept his hands to himself, but Toby and Roman were only too happy to lift Holden's arms for him and slam them on the desk.

From where he sat, Carver smiled into Holden's eyes while he examined the inmate's hands.

"You have rather large, capable hands, Holden. Calloused, working hands, scored with burns and—bite marks too. Hmm! Yet they were always clean, meticulously scrubbed. Why is that, Holden? You don't suffer from any compulsion to always wash them. But old habits die hard, don't they? Even if you don't work here anymore..."

Carver stopped turning the hands over, his attention fixed on the thin red stains along the fingernails, and began rubbing them with his thumb before Holden snatched his hands back.

The doctor chuckled at that. "After all, you were caught poisoning my patients, thinking you might 'cure' them from some imaginary ailment. You always washed your hands afterwards—that was your tell."

Still smiling, Carver retrieved the brown bottle, and shook

out three gelatinous red capsules into his open palm. Toby, Roman, and the presently absent Samson's methods had yielded no results; they may have worked on the other inmates, but Holden was numb as a rock on—at least the outside. No, it required a surgical touch, and being a skilled practitioner, Carver knew which nerve to pluck: already the inmate had lost his smug expression and was following Carver's hands as the doctor lined up the capsules on his desk.

"You know, I'm concerned about the well-being of our patients—our family, I should say. I'll do whatever it takes to return them safely into the fold. Those that wandered off will return," he said, pressing his thumb down on one of the capsules until it exploded into a red splatter under the pressure.

Holden glared at Carver.

"But there is one inmate that concerns me more than the others, at the moment: an inmate that had gone missing just before this mess." He squished another capsule with his thumb.

Holden lunged forward but was held back by the orderlies.

"Therefore, I ask you, Holden, while you still have use of your tongue," Carver pressed down on the third capsule without damaging it, "where is he?"

CHAPTER 8

"Well, that could have gone better. Things went south the moment they brought you back. As always, I went off half-cocked and tried to take matters into my hands. But I had no choice. I know there's a narrow window before those capsules are ineffective, and if I didn't reach you on time—

"Anyway, I thought I'd scare them off to clear the way. It went about as well as you might imagine. But then three of them showed up and it got ugly…

"Then I found you in the lobby, and you looked so far gone I almost put an end to you like we'd agreed. But I couldn't bring myself to do it. So, I brought you here and gave you another dose—had to practically force it down your throat this time—almost cost me a finger, but it should be enough to stabilize your condition for now. I think. I know it's not how it's supposed to work, but it's better than nothing.

"I'm keeping the gun for now. To be honest, I'd rather not have it on me, but I can't risk leaving it with you. I'll return it to you once I'm sure you're of sound mind again. I managed to smuggle in your Skins and some coveralls to conceal them. Also, I've modified the scissors you had on you, should you need to use them. Do what you have to do, and come find me later. But don't take your sweet time, or you might as well use those knives against yourself."

"Greg here. And just before me was the entirety of a recorded message I found playing for me not long after I woke up in a bathtub. I can't explain that one—my head's still reeling trying to answer a few questions, like, say: what the hell is this guy talking about? More importantly, what the hell did he dose me with? To stabilize what? Should I just be happy he didn't put an end to me 'like we'd agreed?' I'm getting shades of a murder-suicide pact here. He spoke like he knew me. Guess he thinks I'm his missing friend. Unfortunately, the gentleman left before I could correct him—not that I'm eager to tell him that the slippery bastard ran off without him.

"Right now, I'm standing in the adjacent room, and I can see a few items laid out on a table: the coveralls he mentioned; the penlight and large scissors I found in the lobby, which I didn't recognize at first because he'd unscrewed the blades, wrapped the handle of each with strips of cloth, and basically turned them into shivs. Very thoughtful of him. There's also a small bag of—what's this? Jerky? Yeah, it looks like jerky—venison, I think… Anyway, I'd assumed they were the 'skins' he mentioned—'skins' being his cute name for jerky. But there's this—this— (ahem) Excuse me. Instead I find—"

Greg almost dropped the recorder setting it down on the table. He pressed a hand over his mouth against a sudden reflux in the back of his throat. The tired, blueish glow from the fluorescent light mounted over a small mirror and dresser had been increasingly irritating to his eyes, inducing a sickening headache that had been ebbing and flowing ever since he woke up. Or it might have been the smell of jerky that exacerbated his nausea.

At any rate, he bolted for the bathroom in time to bend over the sink, heaving and coughing, almost choking for a second or two, until something dislodged itself from his throat and he violently spat the wet lump into the shallow bowl.

He paused to recover, trying to catch his breath between coughs, spitting again to jettison a mucous string of saliva. Through tear-blurred eyes he glanced down at what he thought was a gob of bloodied phlegm. Daze turned to uncertainty while he blinked to clear his vision, and there was only a brief moment to form a quick impression of something pale that curled upon itself—eyeless and languidly writhing—before the knot of flesh, in its blood-slicked momentum, slipped and fell down the sink's hole.

A string of shaky breaths sputtered from his mouth as he stared at the red smear trailing down the curve of the sink bowl, not sure whether to remain petrified in place or peer into the sink's gullet to see if something was wedged down there.

He staggered back and almost fell into the tub behind him, then turned and ran the water from the tub's faucet and began frantically rinsing out his mouth, until the water he spat came out clear. The water was icy enough to frost the faucet, and though he was numb in his wet clothes, Greg still leaned in to the hand that cupped the running water, drinking thirstily.

With dragging steps, he returned to the table, took the recorder, and slumped on the floor with his back to the wall.

He lifted the device to his mouth, pressed the record button, and then froze.

Several seconds passed while he sat with the recorder held close to his lips and nothing to capture but stalled breath; his red-rimmed eyes searched the empty space before them for the catalyst phrase that would undo the knot of thoughts and string along a coherent narrative of what had happened.

"Greg here," and "I–uh—was sick just now…" was all he managed before doubt overtook him and checked any ensuing elaboration. After all… after all, he could be mistaken in what he saw, or thought he saw, though somehow doubt was less assuring, if not worse than certainty. Each revisit seemed to muddle his memory of that brief moment: sometimes it was a mere glob of phlegm; sometimes it was not…

"I threw up something into the sink, but I couldn't see what it was."

Because it skated down the drain.

A hoarse chuckle escaped his throat as he smiled helplessly, then clamped his free hand over his mouth to stifle the sound and stop himself from further hysterics.

At length, the odd giddiness ebbed away, and he sat quietly, his head leaned back against the wall.

The bathroom door was open before him, its interior white and pristine in the filtered sunlight. Out of bright ideas, he thought a shower would help clear his head. There was still a supply of hot water left, and through the rising steam, Greg removed the sodden coveralls—the sleeve sucking hatefully at his arm as he peeled it off—then ducked his head under the shower nozzle, letting the running water wash away the glaze of sweat and with it any vague sense of contamination.

Later, after the water had run cold, Greg stepped into the blue twilight of the adjacent room, calm and alert, rending a strip of jerky with his teeth and chewing it thoughtfully while eyeing the other items on the table.

The improvised weapons were of interest, but more intriguing was the black outfit, which he held up for scrutiny.

It resembled a wetsuit with a high collar and protective padding on the outside paneled to vaguely mimic torso muscles. The arms and legs were likewise padded, though some of the panels doubled as pockets. But for all that, the suit had a sleek appearance, in part due to the material, which had a fine, scaly texture reminiscent of snakeskin, albeit thicker.

"I guess these are so-called Skins," Greg remarked, squinting quizzically, turning it over and partially inside out, looking for an emblem or insignia and wondering whether it was tactical gear, or some sort of high-end activewear.

"Not even a laundry tag," he muttered, laying it flat on the table to unfasten the bias zipper that ran from its left shoulder, across the middle, and stopped over the right hip.

"Skins" was an apt name for it: it had a close fit, lined inwardly as well, compressing the back of his neck, lumbar and stomach; and yet the leathery material stretched and allowed him to comfortably lift his legs, reach over his shoulders, and crouch without constraint. The high collar, too, covered his throat without any stifling pressure.

Before the small mirror, Greg lifted his chin and did a couple of half-turns, appraising his appearance, at which he raised his eyebrows in a mix of mild surprise and approval.

The reflection frowned back from a mirrored room with the

same tired blue florescent light overhead that dusted his inky shoulders with an insectile gleam like a beetle's shell.

Something wasn't right: the high collar covered most of his neck, but now it reached his jawline and chin. The shadows melted the line between his own skin and the suit. He leaned in for closer scrutiny, then he tipped his head and started back when he saw the fine, diamond-shaped scales growing out of the suit that were now embedded with his jaw.

But just as he touched his throat, the absurd vision was gone, and he stood staring at himself in flabbergasted silence. The collar was no longer melded to him—he slipped two fingers into it to make sure he could pry it loose.

No, of course not; it was just a play of shadow and light. Or so he kept repeating to himself as he stepped into the dry coveralls and closed them over the Skins.

CHAPTER 9

Having slept until he could not sleep anymore, the boy lay on his side in the darkness, wide awake, his ear pressed to the floor, listening to any sound that might be carried to him from any part of the house. The perpetual hum was sometimes punctured by a muffled clank or creak, small incidental sounds that did not signify movement, but meant that the sleepy, empty house was still occupied, with running pipes and cables for bowels and veins—alive in its own way. It was easier to track the hours on a clear day, when the sunlight would slant through the windows in the room and make a thin radiant line under the closet door.

But days like today, when the sky was leaden and grey, and evening overtook the afternoon hours, the line of light under the door would barely be there for him to read.

From this small space, he heard the wind blow, whistling through the hairline cracks. Both sorrowful and comforting, it drowned out the other sounds he heard, sounds he could not place, and which sometimes came to him when he was left alone for the day with no one to talk to.

There were times when the hours seemed to stretch into days, and this was one of those times. They could not have been gone for over a day; the switch always happened at the end of the day. That was the arrangement.

But while he remained awake, the distant sound of the front door never came, and after an immeasurable time, his eyes closed of their own accord.

Greg stepped out into a dark hallway. Much like the room he emerged from, it seemed long abandoned to dust, and he surmised from the bare white walls and warped wooden floor that he was in some neglected corner of the building. Or so he thought, until he turned a corner and found himself looking down a hallway lined with doors that stood ajar, spilling rich, yellow light into the unlit corridor.

He hesitated, expecting to find someone entering or exiting one of the rooms. But after observing the prevalent silence, which he took to be a sign of vacancy, he stole down the corridor, looking left and right, and catching glimpses of the small empty rooms as he passed them by.

Though modestly furnished with wooden beds and dressers, the rooms looked to be in dire need of housekeeping; and likely their owners expected someone to tidy up after them, leaving their beds unmade, their dresser drawers gaping open, and their discarded uniforms strewn across the floor.

That last item confirmed Greg's suspicion that he was in

the staff's living quarters, and he began to wonder whether the inmate had gunned down the staff left and right before bringing him here. The thought was absurd, more so since no bodies were to be seen, though the question remained why the inmate had brought him here. Even if there was such a thing as hiding in plain sight, and the orderlies might not consider looking for them here, they still risked getting caught as soon as either of them left the room. Then again, this was the same inmate responsible for killing three orderlies; and Greg, now staring down at one of the makeshift knives he had in hand, wondered whether he was expected to do the same should he encounter anyone. Suddenly there was new meaning behind the inmate's: "Do what you have to do."

For a moment, Greg debated whether it was better to keep the knife at the ready, or get rid of it and its mate, which he kept hidden in the Skin's thigh pocket. It's true he wanted nothing to do with the inmate's killing spree, but then again, he might not have to use it: the sight of the sharp blade alone would keep anyone at a distance. Even the orderlies, regardless of their size, would hesitate to come after him. He could hold his own in an unarmed fight, but against three or more orderlies, he needed an edge, so to speak.

Having settled on keeping the knife, Greg looked at it again, appreciating its reassuring weight in his palm when a loud thump sounded above him.

Greg flashed the penlight up at the ceiling, sweeping it every which way expecting to find hairline cracks in the plaster. But the stark white plaster showed a smooth surface, albeit threaded with wisps of ruined cobwebs.

Again came the thump, followed by a long rasp, like something dragging across the floor above. It went on in that succession: thump-rasp, thump-rasp, which faded as the sound traveled away from him.

Then he heard something else, a muffled shout or cry coming from a few doors down. Someone was there, after all.

He crept along the wall, holding the makeshift weapon—seven inches long and razor sharp—enough to make a point without the need to draw blood, he hoped. Twice he had to pause after the warped floorboards underfoot gave a creak, but eventually he stopped and crouched in front of a door that stood ajar, through which he suspected the noise originated.

The light painted an orange streak down one side of his face, irradiating one eye that looked in from under a lowered brow, its now pale iris sliding imperceptibly up, right, down, and left, trying to take in the whole room through the narrow opening.

A man stood in one corner of the room facing the wall: lofty, corpulent, florid in his white underwear. Though Greg only saw the back of the shaved head resting on rolls of neck fat, he recognized him as one of three orderlies that made up his welcome committee, and the largest of the happy trio at that: it was hard to misidentify a person who needed to duck his head coming through the door and seemed capable of bench pressing a small car.

The irony in their reversed situation did not escape Greg, even if the orderly was not aware of being watched—at least not yet. Then Greg noticed the bed with the disheveled linen near the orderly, and the arm that was draped across the bed, which was hard to see at first due to the heaped-up bedsheets. The rest of the body was hidden from view, half-sprawled on the floor in that cramped space between the bed and the wall, as if the owner of the arm had tried to crawl away but lost consciousness in the midst of it.

The sight absorbed Greg into lingering longer than he should have, and realizing this, he shifted his gaze back at the orderly, almost expecting him to intuit his presence and turn around. But the orderly remained where he was, fixed and idle as a statue, unaccountably facing the corner. Several seconds passed with an ever-growing sense of oppression that came from the stillness. But when it seemed the orderly was not going to move any time soon, Greg raised himself and, half-crouching, backed away with his eyes on the door until he reached a shadowy patch, where he turned and stole away.

Behind him, a laugh rippled through the air, like a trickle of ice water.

Greg wheeled around, glaring in the dark and brandishing the knife before him.

The orderly now stood in the middle of the hallway with only enough light behind him to outline his monolithic frame, leaving his face black and unreadable.

Unsure whether or not the orderly had seen him, Greg took a step back, withdrawing deeper into the shadows but keeping the knife upheld, in case the orderly could see him.

When nothing happened, Greg took another step, and the warped floorboard under him gave a crisp snap.

Without warning, the orderly launched himself, swallowing the distance between them in a few giant steps.

Greg swore, turned tail, and ran.

Within the folds of the shadows was the question of whether he dared use his penlight and risk revealing his position to the orderly, or keep fumbling his way through the dark.

Presently, Greg crouched against the wall, chest heaving as he tried to catch his breath without making a sound, listening to the orderly moving around somewhere nearby.

At least right now he's as blind as I am, thought Greg, shutting his eyes for a moment, trying to get them adjusted to the dark, at the same time hoping the orderly would give up and move on elsewhere.

Inwardly, he kicked himself for falling back at the decisive moment instead of fighting back, never mind that he was startled into retreat by the giant hurtling towards him. Moreover, he froze at the crucial moment: never having drawn a sharp weapon on anyone before, and, regardless of the animosity he felt towards the orderly, a part of him hesitated at the thought of stabbing someone. Still, he stubbornly maintained that his retreat was a strategic fall back rather than acknowledge his squeamish side. Yet now revisited him the odor of blood and offal from the aftermath of the shooting in the hallway, and his elevated pulse hammered steadily in his ears as he opened his eyes to the staring corpse lying prone at his feet, rising and falling in a subtle motion, as if it were breathing.

From his left came the faintest stir of air that followed the muted shuffling of footsteps, before the orderly's fingers brushed the top of Greg's head. The orderly had time to lay his hand on Greg's head, meaning to clench a handful of hair, before the latter swung his right arm in an upward arc, sinking the knife's point into the orderly's forearm.

The orderly howled at the injury, and fell back, nursing his arm. Greg stumbled forward, recovered his footing, but did not reach far before the orderly caught him by the back of his coveralls, wrapped one arm across his neck, hooked the other under his leg, and so heaved Greg up and threw him against the wall.

Greg bounced off, landed on his back, and got the air

knocked out of him. He grabbed his lower back with his free hand, uncontrollably wheezing as he rolled over to stretch out on hand and knees, wanting to open up his lungs. Around him, the pitch-black surroundings whirled maniacally, and while he was absorbed with trying to breathe again, the orderly had ambled over, grabbed Greg by the ankles, and began to drag him away facedown.

After thirty seconds had passed—brief in measured ticks, eternal in the absence of air—Greg's diaphragm unclenched and allowed his lungs to fill with air. It took him a few seconds more to recover enough to survey the relatively brighter surroundings and realize he was being taken back to the orderly's room. He clambered and clawed the cracked floorboards, fruitlessly trying to grab onto anything.

The orderly had regained his room, and was about to pull his victim through the door, when he discovered the body he had been dragging effortlessly was now anchored in place.

Moments earlier, Greg had essayed using the knife to brake their movement, stabbing the floor with it and almost losing it as it skidded and bounced off the hard surface, until the blade's sharp edge got caught in a deep crack between two boards. And feeling it affixed to the ground like a tent stake, Greg lashed his other hand around the fist that closed over the knife, pulling himself toward it. If the blade cut into his palms or fingers, the pain did not register. All that mattered was that they stopped now.

Unable to see what had happened, the orderly leaned forward for a better look, inadvertently relaxing his grip on Greg's ankles, allowing him to snatch one leg free and a throw a sound kick to the orderly's stomach.

The orderly staggered back, and with both legs now free,

Greg rolled over onto his back to deliver a few more kicks when someone hooked their arms under his and dragged him away.

This newcomer then pulled Greg up to his feet, and thinking he was being attacked, Greg turned on him, wrapped his arms around the other person's waist and slammed him against the wall.

"Clark, stop, it's me!" called the newcomer, encircling Greg's arms with his own to stop the attack without making any move to retaliate.

On hearing the young-sounding voice, Greg released him and stepped back. The two of them stood for a confused moment in the semi-dark, Greg observing the grey coveralls worn by the younger inmate, who himself seemed surprised on seeing Greg's face. Both had forgotten the red-faced orderly until they heard him roar in anger as he rose to his feet, signaling their cue to run.

CHAPTER 10

They stood catching their breath, having run until they put a decent distance between them and the orderly.

The inmate, after sticking his head out of the door to reaffirm that they were not being pursued, turned to Greg. "Who are you?"

"What's it to you?" retaliated Greg, between breaths. He winced after the inmate pulled a cord and flooded the small storeroom with light from a naked bulb.

"You might want to turn that off before it gets someone's attention."

"Then I won't see," quietly protested the inmate, a sloe-eyed, skinny kid who looked to be on the cusp of his twenties.

"I have a penlight, it should be enough."

The inmate waited until Greg pulled out the penlight, turned it on, and placed it on the dusty steel shelving unit between them before he killed the light on his end.

One of his hands felt wet, and in the white glow of his

penlight, Greg saw it had sustained a cut across the palm and was bleeding, while the other hand suffered little more than a red indentation.

He approached a small sink installed in one corner, nerving himself to the imminent sting as he turned the faucet before sticking his hand under the running water. The cut did not sting, however, and with mild wonder, he rotated his hand through the cold stream, letting it wash over his palm, then knuckles, then palm again. The first aid box mounted by the sink offered little more than a thin roll of gauze and a spool of surgical tape; but he made do by folding the former into a wad, pressing it into the cut, and winding the tape a few times around his hand to secure it.

All through this, the inmate had thankfully exhibited good sense by remaining silent; the last thing Greg wanted, as he tore the tape, flexed his hand, and noticed that both hands were vexed with tremors—the last thing he wanted was to be interrogated, let alone engage in small talk.

Having dressed the cut, Greg leaned against a wooden crate, undid the coveralls, and reached under them for the Skins pocket that held his recorder—examining it, turning it over to check for damage, and shaking it close to his ear to hear if anything loose rattled inside. Satisfied it seemed intact, he returned it, and gave his leg a cursory pat to check the other knife was still in its pocket, when he caught the inmate suspiciously eyeing him.

The inmate cleared his throat and tilted his chin to indicate the black suit.

"Couldn't help noticing that thing you're wearing—it's not exactly standard issue here," he said, and when Greg gave no response, he went on: "Are you working with that man?"

"What man?" asked Greg. "Given the population here, you'll have to be more specific."

"Fine: an inmate—middle-aged, tall—sort of brawny—passed by here earlier..." he trailed off. "Never mind. I guess it doesn't ring any bells."

"No, go on," said Greg, but received no answer from the inmate, who turned to rummage through the laden shelves, isolating boxes of food ready to eat from dry ingredients. He came across a box of chocolate wafers and seemed in awe of his find until Greg snatched it from his hand.

"You want them?" he asked, rattling the box. "Start talking."

The inmate looked from him to the box, then gave a disdainful snort. "Whatever."

"Suit yourself," said Greg, opening the box and biting into one. "Hmm—not bad. They sort of melt in your mouth. Better than I remember. Then again, after a diet of slop, I bet everything tastes better—" he paused, frowning at the small mountain of food the inmate was accumulating. "Hell, boy, you got orphans to feed or something?"

The inmate spared him a look, then moved to another corner and pretended to be too busy searching for something to carry the food he gathered to notice Greg, who inched closer and started on another wafer.

"You know," he said, glancing at the pile of food the inmate had gathered, "I bet something salty would go great with these. I see you got a bag of chips there—"

The inmate dashed in sideways to intercept him. "Look, what do you want? I said I don't know anything."

"Bullshit. We all know something."

"Yeah?" chuckled the inmate. "Well, I'm sure you don't

need me to tell you something is seriously off with this place, and I'm not talking about this cult-like program."

Greg studied him a moment, offered the box of wafers, but kept hold of it when the inmate tried to take it.

"Did he have a gun?" asked Greg.

The young inmate paused to consider. "No—I don't know. If he did, I didn't see it."

Greg released the box to reach for the handheld recorder. "Did he sound something like this?" He played back a short sample of the message.

"I—guess that was him," said the inmate, sounding uncertain. "We didn't talk long enough for me to remember his voice."

"What did he say?"

The inmate seemed about to say something, but stopped short of divulging more information than he wanted to, and began packing the food into a battered cardboard box. "Listen, it's nothing personal, but I don't know who you are and who to trust at this point—"

"I'm Greg."

"Nader," muttered the inmate dismissively. "Look, Greg, I'm sorry but I really need to go."

"I'll come with you then."

"No!"

"Why not?"

"Because—" Nader floundered for an excuse. "Because I can't—invite all and sundry to join us."

"I don't plan on staying. I just want to talk, then I'll be on my way."

"There's nothing to talk about. I already said I don't know

anything."

"Your friends might know something. Besides, you know what would go well with those crackers and biscuits you've got?" said Greg, digging into one of his pockets for the bag of jerky and presenting it with a flourish.

Nader's lips curled with suspicion at the unlabeled plastic bag and the dried strips inside. "What's that?"

"You've never had jerky before?"

"I meant what kind."

"It's meat."

"You mean mystery meat."

"Protein is protein," argued Greg, wagging a reproachful finger. "You want to grow up to be big and strong, you gotta stop being picky."

Nader shook his head with a derisive chuckle. "Oh, no, no—don't go thinking you can bribe me with dog treats."

As soon as he managed to lift the cardboard, the bottom gave out, spilling its contents on the floor. Greg watched a few cans roll by before turning to Nader, who still held the collapsed box with a vacant look of exasperation.

"You need help with that?"

"Forget it, it's surplus," said Nader, stooping to pick up whatever he could and left carrying a heap in his arms.

Greg retrieved the penlight, picked up one of the cans, and caught up with Nader in the hallway.

"Stop following me!"

"But I've got meat and—" Greg turned over the can to check the label before calling after him—"hey, peaches!"

It was not long before Nader stopped protesting Greg's company. And while he was in no position to shake him off, it helped that Greg carried a penlight, which Nader found useful in finding his way back.

Eventually, they stopped before a series of tapestries draped over a wall.

Nader, hunched over the load he carried, resting his chin on top of the boxes to pin them down, managed a subtle nod to Greg, who stood next to him, cradling more boxes, a few cans, and a large bag of chips in one arm, while the other pointed the light at the tapestry. The woven scenery before him featured ships sailing over an undulating ocean, surrounded by arching whales and leviathans.

At a glance there was nothing remarkable about it, but then the shimmering threads caught Greg's eye, and he frowned as he detected a minute writhing in the lines of the waves. The realization, though delayed by incredulity, soon transfixed him before the animated scene of waves rolling under the ship, monstrous heads rising from the sea, and tails that seemed to perpetually uncoil and dive into the opaque water, yet never entirely disappeared.

Nader nudged his elbow. "Hey—this is not a tour," he hissed. "Push it back."

Greg glanced back at the tapestry, on the verge of asking Nader if he saw it too. But after a second look at the now fixed seascape of the tapestry and its unmoving icons, he said nothing and pushed back the heavy curtain.

Behind it, an old wooden door opened to a slip of a hall that led to a bare, stonewalled room, where the concrete floor pressed hard and cool against their feet.

One of the inmates there lay on the floor, sleeping on a bed of empty burlap bags. Another inmate, a thin man whose flaxen hair fell to his jaw, detached himself from a brooding corner and approached them.

"Well, it's about time," he grumbled. "My back teeth are just about floating here—"

He broke off when he saw Greg, unfolded the arms he had crossed to keep his hands warm, and collared Nader as the boy shuffled by with his load.

"Who's this?"

Nader sighed, half-turned, and said unceremoniously: "Hitch: Greg. Greg? Hitch."

Hitch looked Greg up and down with scrutiny made scornful by the invariably arched eyebrows, hawkish black eyes, and thin, humorless mouth.

"So, you've followed the trail of breadcrumbs all the way here," he said to Greg, eyeing the food he was carrying.

"Not really. I'm just here to get some answers," said Greg, eating a handful of chips from the large bag he carried.

Hitch then spoke to Nader. "What happened to Clark? Or did you trade in one friend for another?"

Nader, now empty-handed, turned an anxious look to Hitch. "Clark's not back?"

A sneer stretched across Hitch's gaunt, bristled face, showing a broken tooth.

"I thought I told you not to split up," he said, looking almost pleased to have caught Nader in a blunder.

"We didn't," said Nader, pacing around as though to retrace his steps. "He was keeping a lookout while I searched the rooms. Then at some point I looked up and he was gone. I couldn't find him anywhere and thought maybe he came back here. But if he never came back—"

He glanced about then started for the door. Hitch moved in to block him.

"Where do you think you're going?"

"To look for Clark."

"Like hell you are. I've been freezing my ass off here while you went and made an ass of yourself back there. You're on watch duty now."

"What about Clark?"

"We'll keep an eye out for him—me and your other friend here," said Hitch, indicating Greg, who was tipping the bag of chips to his mouth and shaking out the last crumbs. "As soon as he's done eating…"

"Or—" said Greg, crumpling the empty bag—"you two could go look while I keep an eye on things here."

Nader looked despondent. "One of us has to stay behind and look after him," he said, glancing at the sleeping inmate covered in burlap, whose only sign of living was a series of wet coughs.

"Why? What's wrong with him?" asked Greg.

"Nothing's wrong!" Hitch interposed, backhanding Nader before he could answer. "And you!" he said, shoving Greg's shoulder, "less talking, more walking if we're going to find this idiot's friend."

"Find him yourself." Greg shoved back.

"Wait, Greg—listen," said Nader, stepping in to interrupt the escalating shoving match, "you want information, right? I'll make it worth your time. I'll tell you everything I know. Everything. Promise. Only please go and look for Clark…"

“Kid, not to sound pessimistic or anything,” said Greg, detaching himself from Nader’s pleading grasp, “but if your friend’s not back by now, and we haven’t seen him on the way here, chances are they might have picked him up already.”

“He could be hiding somewhere—or trapped—maybe one of the room’s door jammed on him and he can’t get out,” said Nader, to which Hitch showed some courtesy by turning away as he laughed to himself.

“Alright,” said Greg with a resigned sigh. “Where did you say you last saw him?”

“One of the rooms in the staff’s quarters—not far from where I found you.”

At that, Greg’s drawn eyebrows relaxed into a look of dread.

“What? What is it?” Nader asked. “You saw something?”

“I don’t know,” answered Greg. “We’ll see.”

CHAPTER 11

Hitch walked two steps behind Greg, maintaining his distance to keep an eye on him in case he tried anything funny.

Trust Nader to pick up this stray, thought Hitch, with a look that threatened to bore holes in the back of Greg's skull. *As if the motherless twit didn't cause enough trouble losing Clark—now he brings in this rat to blow our cover. Didn't even stop to consider the possibility he works for Carver. Then again, the little dumbass never had the pleasure of being snitched on by one of Carver's moles.*

Whether they were inmates or staff in grey, Hitch himself could not tell, but all the same they kept their eyes and ears open to anyone breaking their vow of silence: if they caught inmates whispering or passing notes or even looking significantly at one another, they informed the orderlies keeping watch through a series of subtle looks or gestures; and without warning, the guilty parties would be dragged away. Some had even enticed the inmates to talk, or falsely accused men whose manner or looks they didn't like—an offense for which Hitch himself had paid through the nose.

He glared back at Greg. Of course he was one of Carver's cronies. One, that would explain Clark's disappearance; and two, just look at his uniform. Sure, some inmates wore special armbands on their sleeves after they had reached some stage of enlightenment (if not hopped up on something) and wore that dopey look on their faces. But others were granted a pair of wool socks (amongst other privileges, he assumed) for services rendered to Carver.

But this black garb covering him neck to wrist was new. Probably thermals to keep the damn cold from seeping into his bones like it did with all of them. The shameless bastard didn't even try to hide it, rolling up his coverall sleeves for them to see. Well—wasn't he special? It would have been easy to shake him off if that idiot hadn't brought him to their hiding spot. It was up to him to get rid of the informer—make sure he didn't get the chance to tell anyone about them and their hiding place…

Greg brushed the back of his head. Though he had passed through the same hallway just minutes ago, it was somewhat changed by the dawn's blue light that now slanted in airy cones through the small, round windows lining one wall of the corridor.

"You know, you're not far from the staff's quarters," he said over his shoulder to Hitch. "How'd you manage to end up here, anyway?"

It was an excuse to check on the inmate without betraying suspicion: he didn't like how Hitch insisted on shadowing him instead of walking by his side.

Hitch said nothing, though Greg caught a glimpse of the scowl he wore as he cut through one of the shafts of light. The look was far from reassuring. Even if he didn't say much, that look said plenty. Still, Greg continued to throw out one question and comment after another, partly to bait him, partly to steal looks over his shoulder at intervals to make sure Hitch maintained that same distance, and if possible, see that he did not bring his hands in front of him with a length of wire or rope or even a strip of coiled cloth between them.

At length, they reached the orderly's room, marked by the abandoned knife, which remained planted in the same spot, firmly lodged between the floorboards. Greg had to waggle the handle several times before he was able to loosen it. Traces of blood laced the blade—whether his or the orderly's, it was hard to say. The narrowness of his escape hit him then, hard and sudden, causing his shoulders to seize up in a belated shudder.

"Well?" Hitch muttered after Greg had stood silent for a few seconds.

Greg cleared his throat. "I passed by here a while back and saw one of the orderlies in this room. I think he had someone with him."

He pointed the penlight at the closed door. The hallway remained unlit, and judging by the absence of the thin line of light from under the closed door, the room was likewise dark.

"And?" asked Hitch, starting to sound impatient. "What did he look like?"

"I don't know. I couldn't see the entire body—just the hand," said Greg, recalling the arm that was sprawled on the bed.

"Oh, there's a telling feature!" scoffed Hitch.

"The lights are off. I doubt anyone's there. But let's just

check to make sure…"

"Well, then—by all means," said Hitch, turning the knob and pushing back the door. "The man with the sharp object goes in first."

Greg glanced at Hitch, then smiled to himself: the petty tyrant was poultry after all.

He shined the light inside and made a quick sweep of the small room.

"Looks clear so far," he said in a low voice, which was true in a sense: he could not see him, but he could not shake off the sense someone was somewhere in the room; he felt a pair of eyes trained on him.

The light switch by the door did not respond.

"Oh, wonderful. Very moody," he said, reaching back to grab Hitch by the elbow, guiding him to stay at his side as he entered the room rather than linger behind, where he could easily run off at the first sign of danger—maybe even shove him in harm's way.

Hitch side-glanced at Greg with a faint sneer: the milquetoast had a knife *and* a flashlight, and *still* wanted to hold hands before stepping into a dark room.

The single bed waxed stark and pale in the glare of the flashlight, and the shadows retreated into the folds of the rumpled sheets; but that was all they could find: both bed and the floor around it were empty.

"There was a body here," said Greg, pointing to the nook between the wall and the bed.

"It's gone now," said Hitch with the finality of kicking dirt into an open grave.

Greg crouched to examine a glistening streak that began

at the floor of the nook, traveled up the wall, and stopped at the rectangular mouth of an open air shaft, as if someone had dragged a wet mop there, leaving a moist trail that was starting to dry up.

"Are we done here?" demanded Hitch.

Without taking his eyes off the vent, Greg raised a hand to silence him. "Shh! Listen."

Hitch followed his gaze up to the shaft: though its grille cover was missing, it seemed too narrow for anyone to crawl through, and too high to climb into without a ladder; no piece of furniture had been pushed against the wall to aid in climbing to the vent.

He gave a disdainful chuckle. "Oh, I see. He scaled up the walls and crawled in there, right?"

Greg ignored him and began pushing the single bed towards the wall with the open vent. He then reached up, trying to tuck the handheld recorder into the shaft and capture the sound that was coming through it. But even as he stood on the bed on tiptoe, he could barely touch the edge of the gaping shaft.

At that moment, Hitch saw an opportunity, and grinned to himself as he grabbed a nearby chair.

"Here, let me," he said, setting the chair on the bed.

Greg seemed puzzled by this unexpected gesture, but only hesitated a moment before climbing onto the chair. Hitch meanwhile kept his head bowed between his extended arms, pretending to be engrossed in steadying the chair to conceal a widening grin, anticipating the moment in which he'd pull the chair from under the idiot and let him fall—with luck, breaking his neck. And if he managed to land unharmed, Hitch would still have time to dash the chair against his head. An eye for an eye, and a brutal end to the informer.

"Keep it steady," said Greg just over a whisper, starting the recorder and clasping the edge of the shaft's mouth to further stabilize his wobbling perch. His head was a few inches short of the opening, but he was able to reach his hand inside the shaft a little, pushing the recorder as close as possible to the source of sound.

A minute ago he had caught only hints of it, like an electric hum. Now he heard it better, even if it was still somewhat faint: a feminine singing voice coming from the depths of the vent. The distance clouded the words, as did the echoes, and all he could catch was a series of incoherent syllables. Her silvery voice rose to a high note that cracked into a shrill, serrated screech that then trailed into a long wheeze. It started again: strong and smooth, rising into a high clear note only to break into a hoarse wail that disintegrated into a long, raspy, thin hum, full of *n* sounds, as though the singer was suddenly exhausted or suffering some deep, visceral pain.

It had a strange effect on him, this lone, distant voice echoing through the shaft: it made him flush with heat, and then his blood ran cold; he wanted to dive from his high post and out the room in one bounding leap; at the same time he wanted, against his better judgement, to pull himself up and climb into the vent. His horror was appropriate, though he could not explain his other impulse any more than he could explain what he was hearing. But above all, he was so taken by it that he had forgotten where he was and what brought him here, until the chair began to totter underfoot. He glanced down, and was about to tell Hitch to keep the chair steady when, from the depths of the narrow vent shaft, something reached out, drawn by the recorder's small red light, and brushed against his hand.

It was a light touch, but it startled Greg, and he overbalanced and fell back.

A few seconds earlier, Hitch had been stuck in his position, holding the chair with tense arms and clammy hands, trying to induce himself to snatch it away. It was a simple enough plan in theory, but like the tablecloth trick, carrying it out in reality revealed how formidable and ticklish the procedure was. For one thing, the chair sank into the bed under Greg's weight, who moreover held on to the edge of the shaft for added stability. Even if he managed to pull the chair, the drop seemed less fatal now. And what if Greg realized something was off beforehand and jumped down before Hitch managed to drop him; what if he toppled over the wrong way and landed on him; what if he—

The tortured string of questions broke with Greg tumbling back and falling on top of Hitch.

They lay in an awkward pile, Greg with his feet splayed on the bed and the rest of him on the floor, and Hitch pinned under him, both men groaning in pain, convinced they broke something.

Then Hitch, grumbling, dragged himself from under Greg, who seemed oblivious to the other man's complaints, keeping his gaze fixed on the vent as he rolled onto his side. His hand fell on the penlight, and he shone it on the narrow opening, but found little there apart from spores of dust winking in the light.

Soapy water swirled down the large sink in a bright room, where Carver stood scrubbing his hands up to the elbows.

“Holden’s asleep?” he said, addressing the middle-aged nurse who stood behind him. “Good. Keep him under watch and don’t remove that gag. You never know when he might wake up and try to chew his tongue off again—without so much as a blink.”

His eyes followed the streaming water, but his vision had taken an inward slant, and he stood still, reflecting for a moment.

“We won’t get anything out of him. Though I wonder whether our new friend might help… Samson tells me he last saw him wandering the staff’s quarters—not far from where they picked up Holden. But there are signs of infestation. We’ll just have to wait until they emerge from there. I’m sure Wyatt will manage it. In the meantime, tell everyone that the area is off limits.”

CHAPTER 12

Having failed their search, Hitch and Greg made their way back to the shelter carrying pillows and blankets. And while they peeked into every room on their way back, the results were the same regardless.

Greg remained distracted by his thoughts, and Hitch, after a momentary relief that his intentions were not yet exposed, maintained a morose silence, brooding over his next move.

Upon entering the shelter, they found Nader cradling the sleeping inmate's head on his knees, his hand poised over the head, pinching something between his fingers until a few drops fell into the inmate's open mouth. Though his head was uncovered now, Greg saw it was still partially bandaged or bound by a blindfold, and his gaze traveled from the head to the red-stained fingers suspended over them to Nader's look of surprise tinged with guilt.

Hitch, throwing the pillows and covers aside, caught Nader by the front of his uniform.

"The hell you think you're doing, boy, huh?" he breathed menacingly, giving Nader a jolting shake.

"I wanted to—wanted to wake him up," stammered the other, a glint of fear in his widening eyes. "He was running a fever and I didn't know what to do, so I gave him this."

He held up something small and berry-like, crushed between his thumb and forefinger.

"What did you just give him?" demanded Hitch, twisting his hands, which held fistfuls of Nader's shirt to pull him closer. The blindfolded inmate's head slid off Nader's lap as he was forced to rise to his feet.

"It's medicine, I swear! An inmate gave them to me."

"An inmate," repeated Hitch, and began to turn to Greg when Nader said: "Not him—this other guy I met outside."

"You have five seconds to start making sense, boy," said Hitch with a glare that showed more white around his black irises.

"I met this inmate back in the hallway, after Clark disappeared—he gave me these capsules—asked me to take one of these and hand the rest out to everyone—said it was important. I took one awhile back and I've felt fine. So I thought I'd give one to Wyatt..."

"One of what? Of what, boy?" Again, he shook Nader with each inquiry. "Where is this inmate, huh? We turned the apartments inside out looking for your idiot friend while you sat here playing doctor, giving him God-knows-what—I swear if something happens to him, and you sabotage this, so help me, I'll paint the floor with you—"

"You might want to step back yourself if you don't want to stomp the poor guy's head," warned Greg, placing an arresting hand on Hitch to keep him from accidentally treading on the unconscious inmate.

Hitch kept his eyes fixed on Nader, though he was starting to become aware of the bandaged head at his feet. A couple of seconds later he released Nader with a shove.

"Let me see that," said Greg, extending his hand to Nader.

"I'm telling you, I took one and I felt fine," reiterated Nader, now expressing a slight tremble in his voice as he pulled down and readjusted the front of his coveralls.

Meanwhile Greg examined the crushed red capsule in his bandaged palm, turning it over with his fingertips. Something about it and the whole weird scene he had walked in on scratched at the back of his mind with a strange familiarity.

"No side effects or anything," Nader went on. "It had a weird aftertaste, but that was it. He's been asleep for a while now and wouldn't respond when I tried to wake him up. And his forehead felt hot—"

"You said an inmate gave these to you," said Greg. "Would that be the same inmate you mentioned awhile back?"

"Yeah, same guy."

"What are these capsules?"

Nader shrugged. "Could be NSAID, or an antidote, or some kind of medication. Maybe there's something going around like malaria..."

The crushed capsule in Greg's hand left a red smudge on his palm, much like the stains on Nader's fingers. His mind traveled back to the tub in the bathroom where he had woken up with remnants of a dream that by now had all but faded into grainy impressions; the memory of the lump that fell into the sink, however, was still fresh in his mind.

"You didn't feel anything? Anything at all?" he inquired, grabbing Nader by the shoulders, and the boy thought, *here we go,* assuming Greg was going to continue where Hitch had left off.

"I swear, I felt nothing. At least nothing like nausea, skin rash, or a headache or anything."

The answer confused Greg more than it had assured its owner, who craned his neck and looked about the room.

"What happened to Clark?"

For a moment the question baffled Greg. Then he remembered the reason they went out and shook his head.

"I'm sorry. We checked everywhere, but we couldn't find him."

Nader looked crestfallen but gave a steadfast nod: "I'll find him. If they got him, I'll find a way to get him out."

Greg said nothing but fetched the pillow, cover, and blanket, made a modest bed on the concrete floor, then motioned Nader to help him lay the comatose inmate on it. Hitch stood with his hands on his hips, neither protesting nor helping, but observing them in the hapless attitude of one watching his wrecked car getting towed away.

Shortly thereafter, Greg sat cross-legged on his makeshift bed with a blanket draped over his shoulders, facing Nader, who likewise sat on his own bed two feet away. Hitch had picked a corner near the sleeping inmate, piled burlap sacks into a nest, covered them with the bedspread, and now reclined like a petulant lord, pecking at an open can of candied nuts.

Greg had lined small jars that contained a medley of preserves and honey in front of him and was experimentally dipping saltine crackers into each jar. Nader on his part had smuggled the box of chocolate wafers under his blanket, and though secure in the knowledge that Hitch couldn't see him, still ate in a furtive manner.

"I never understood the whole sweet-and-savory thing," said Nader, watching Greg bite into a cracker dipped in honey with ill-disguised distaste.

"You just haven't found the right combination of things," answered Greg, pausing to consider the taste before shrugging it off as tolerable. "Everything tastes better with the right sauce. Trust me, stock up on those take-out condiments, and you can turn cheap ingredients into something as good as gourmet, if not better. Even leftovers are more interesting when they have that delicate, ineffable 'je-ne-say-qwah' flavor."

Nader looked unconvinced, and declined Greg's enthusiastic offer to try saltine and strawberry jam.

"Your loss," said Greg, taking a bite of it himself, and rolling his eyes in rapture at the combination. "Anyway, you were going to tell me about this inmate…"

"Right," said Nader, glad for the change of subject. "I met him after Clark had disappeared. We were in one of the rooms and I was searching under the bed for anything of value—you know, cash hidden under the mattress and whatnot. Clark was supposed to be the lookout, but when I looked up, he was gone, and the door was wide open. I went into the hallway to look for him, and that's when I ran into him—the inmate, I mean. At first I thought it was one of the orderlies, but he was wearing grey, like us. He asked if anyone was with me and I said no—which was true at the time, but I didn't know if I could trust him, you know? Anyway, he doesn't buy it, but he's not offended or anything—he just gave me these and told me to take one."

Here Nader drew out a folded piece of paper from his rolled-up sleeve, opened it, and laid it on the floor between them with the gravity of presenting a relic. Two red capsules sat in the center of the creased paper, glowing softly under the slope of white light filtering through the narrow window. "There were four capsules, but I took one and—well, you saw me give the other to Wyatt there," said Nader, glancing over his shoulder at the sleeping inmate.

"Did he tell you what they are or what they're for?" said Greg, returning to the capsules.

"And did your mama never warn you 'bout taking candy from strangers?" Hitch piped up behind Nader, pelting him with an almond.

Nader, ignoring Hitch, went on: "He didn't get the chance to. We were standing in the hallway, and out of nowhere he stopped talking and shoved me into the room. I was surprised at first, but when I saw two orderlies run past the open door going after him, I understood why. I guess they didn't notice me because they just ran straight for him. I hid until I was sure the coast was clear; that's when I took the capsule."

"Just like that? Without knowing what they're for?"

"Yeah."

Greg shook his head in a reproachful manner, which Nader received as one would an approving slap on the back for pulling a stunt: he smiled with conscious pride and gave a careless shrug.

"I mean, the guy saved me from getting caught, so I owe him the benefit of the doubt. They might be important; I couldn't throw them away any more than push them onto the others without testing them first. See, I come from a family of doctors and chemists—was studying to get into the field—"

"Oh-ho-ho!" laughed Hitch in disbelief, tossing another almond. "That doesn't even begin to qualify you to be a pharmacist!"

"I guess not. But right now, we're not living in a normal society with access to drugstores or meds."

"Sure, Pollyanna. Just don't come crying to me when those pills turn out to be laxatives or something."

"Yeah, you just keep picking through those nuts, Hitch, maybe you'll find your brain in there," muttered Nader in an aside.

Greg, reflecting back on the vomiting episode that followed him waking up in the bathroom, added: "He's right. What if it was a purgative of some sort?"

Nader dismissed the suggestion at first: "If it were, I'd have felt something by now—" then paled a little—"unless it's slow-acting. God, I hope not! I could make quick runs for the staff's rooms to use their bathrooms, so long as the area is deserted. But if they come back—I'd rather not be found shackled to the toilet seat when they do."

Greg smiled wryly, but not without sympathy. "You might want to get yourself a bucket if you plan on staying here awhile."

"That's the thing: we weren't planning on staying here. We just ducked in here soon after the chaos began. Wyatt showed us this place, told us we could hide here until things calmed down. But then he went to sleep and was out cold not long after. We didn't think there was anything wrong at first. Clark and I went to look for provisions while we waited for him to wake up..."

Nader paused to glance back at Hitch and found him dosing open-mouthed with the can of nuts still in his hands; all the same he dropped his voice to a whisper as he elaborated: "See, Wyatt knows a way out without getting caught. He used to work as a janitor here, that's how he knew about this hole in the wall."

"A janitor? So why is he in grey now?"

Nader seemed about to say something, but paused and regarded Greg meditatively, as if he was piecing something together. A strange stillness replaced his bright-eyed look, or perhaps it was nothing more than sleep encroaching upon him. Greg himself had the same drowsy look and bleary vision; the cold had sapped their energy, and what little they ate did nothing to replenish it. The wool blankets, meanwhile, had made them warm and drowsy, yet they both wanted to keep the conversation going, for want of information on Greg's side, and want of talk on Nader's part.

"I didn't get a chance to ask Wyatt," said Nader. "But I'm starting to—see, I have this theory that a lot of us aren't really inmates here..."

Greg bowed his head and yawned, his voice thickening as he spoke through it. "Sure, kid. We're all just prisoners of our collective imagination."

"I'm serious! I mean, why would a janitor become an inmate here? I know *I* haven't been incarcerated here in any official capacity. See, I was a first year med student before I ended up here. There was a case not long ago in which a classmate of mine was killed. I happened to be the last person seen with her, so I was pinned as a prime suspect. I'm innocent, of course, if you'll take my word for it. The night she was killed she just asked me to drop her off somewhere. I don't know her well, but it was late, and she seemed nervous, like someone was after her. So I said yes. The campus security guard saw us, and he's the last person to see her besides me. So, it was his testimony against mine. Investigators kept circling me like sharks. If they couldn't find a lead, I was it. At first I thought I was being paranoid, but then I was set to travel home for the holidays and was told I couldn't leave the country. That's when I began to panic—I mean, you hear of people being incarcerated without conviction. Damned if I stayed, damned if I go? I chose go. I searched and found someone who said he could smuggle me across the border, where I could catch a flight home. I paid that *mother* in *cash!* And all I got was a smooth transition from a truck bed to an iron bed."

At the conclusion, Greg sat quiet for a moment, making a small, contemplative motion with his jaw before nodding. "So, you're saying there's a connection between the two?"

"I don't know. I don't want to go all conspiracy theory on this, but I'm almost sure there's some human trafficking involved here. I mean, what about you? How'd you end up here?"

Greg shifted his heavy-lidded gaze around as he thought it over. "Last thing I remember before waking up here was wandering around this abandoned property in a mountain area—at least, I thought it was abandoned. Dr. Carver says they found me outside, unconscious and in this grey uniform. And, because I happen to share more than a passing resemblance to an escaped inmate, they thought I was him. Carver knows better—not that it helps—he kept me here just so the rest of you wouldn't get any bright ideas and try the same." And sweeping a cursory glance across the hideout, he scoffed: "A lot of good that did him…"

"You believe that story about the escaped inmate?" Nader pursued.

To which Greg exhaled with a sputter. "Man, I don't know what to believe. To be honest, I never bought the story wholesale until I heard your pill-pushing friend talking as if he knew me. You're saying throughout your stay here you've never seen anyone with a face like mine—maybe a creepy, neckbeard twin?"

Nader gave a small shrug. "I never had a chance to take a good look at everyone. I've only been here about a week or so…" he trailed off, then added: "Where are we, by the way?"

"Duncastor."

"Huh—can't say I know where that is. I heard Clark say we're far up north—close to the border, in fact. He said he would help me get across the border if we ever got out."

Greg chuckled at that. "You never learn, do you?"

But Nader remained solemn. "At least I can trust Clark. If it weren't for him, I'd still be back in my cell like all the others."

For a moment, Greg considered asking him what he planned on doing now that Clark was back in his cell; but Nader saved him the trouble by turning in to sleep, ending the conversation. And deciding it was none of his business anyway, Greg lay down and soon slept.

CHAPTER 13

Two figures stood among the pine trees, looming over Greg's head while he lay on the ground. They were covered in black, and they were discussing him. He could not move: a spider was crawling over his closed eyes and he did not wish to provoke it, and so waited until it crept away. It skittered down his face, slinked over his chest and stomach like a snake, and then slid down his side and disappeared.

Then he was in the tub, and a pair of hands moulded themselves over his mouth and under his chin to clamp his jaws shut and force him to swallow whatever it was inside his mouth. He clawed at them and tried to pry them off while he tossed and twisted his head, peeled back his lips, and sputtered red liquid between his teeth before his head jerked forward and he found himself sitting up in bed in the shelter again.

The closed air in the stone walled room was heavy with sleep and steeped in a deep amber light, signifying either the start of the day or the closing of one.

He rubbed the back of his stiff neck, and his hand came back damp with sweat. Sleeping with the Skins on was a mistake. Either that or he was coming down with something: he felt worse waking up than going to bed. His throat was parched, and he tiptoed over the sleeping inmates towards the food pile, opened a can of fruit cocktail, drank the juice, then fished out the fruit cubes and ate them.

As soon as one need was met, another replaced it; his only option was to use one of the bathrooms in the staff's quarters—if they were still vacant. Then again, he was going to leave the relative safety of the shelter anyhow, and it may as well be now than later.

He stopped before the shelter's door to check his belongings were all with him, and while he patted down his pockets, his mind traveled ahead to that room, wondering whether it was still dark and empty, whether he could still hear the voice if he went there again, and whether it would thrill through him in that same disturbing way as it had before.

Both knives were in place, but when he checked the pocket designated to carry the handheld recorder, he found it empty. Suddenly, the uncanny voice, static-ridden and compressed by the small speakers, sang close to him. Greg wheeled around, clapping a hand over his left ear, but found only empty space behind him. Then his eyes focused on a figure several feet behind, sitting in his makeshift bed, outlined by an orange halo of dusky sunlight.

He approached the figure and found it to be the former janitor, who was not only up, but had the handheld recorder and was playing back the recorded audio from the vent. He cocked his head to one side, inclining it toward the device, and listened with a wistful smile as the singing voice broke into a shrill wail, crackling through the small speakers.

"Sweeter than mother's voice, isn't it?" Wyatt asked with a fluttering sigh, raising his blindfolded eyes to Greg. It was hard to place his age: his high, round cheeks and narrow chin were smooth and hairless, and his voice had a thin, boyish quality to it; yet he had a head of severely thinning brown hair through which his scalp shone visible, and there was a middle-aged thickness to his features.

Greg crouched before him and extended his hand, his movements calm and deliberate. Wyatt in turn complied, stopped the tape, and placed the device in Greg's clammy hand.

"You can see," Greg managed to say evenly: the song had stopped, yet still his insubordinate heart kept knocking.

"Whatever filters through the gauze," Wyatt rejoined, tapping his bandaged temple with a sly smile.

"You also make it a habit to go through people's pockets while they sleep?" said Greg, indicating the recorder.

Wyatt raised his palms in a shrug, as though he couldn't help it. "Not many pockets to go through around here." His smile diminished when Greg rose to leave, and without getting up, Wyatt seized Greg's hand in an unexpected show of accuracy.

"That song," he said. "Where did you hear it?"

"That's—some reflex," said Greg, avoiding the question.

The sly smile returned. "I said I can still perceive things, didn't I? Here, let me show you."

Wyatt unclenched Greg's hand, extended the pointer finger, and guided it towards a spot in the center of his bandaged forehead. Done in an instant, the gesture caught Greg off guard, and before he could react, Wyatt had pushed the finger against a soft spot under the bandage, where the skin sank through a hole in his skull.

As soon as that happened, Greg experienced a sharpness of vision in which all the pores of the gauzy bandage had stood out with a harsh clarity, as did the lines on Wyatt's face and between his teeth, and in place of his eyes were blank orbs that seemed about to project out of their sockets into tapering points. It only lasted an instant, but the vision was gone as soon as Greg jerked his hand back. But he remained visibly shaken, staring at the former janitor who basked in his own shadow with a self-satisfied smile.

"Now that we're familiar with each other—" he began, but was cut short when Greg seized him by the lapels.

"Friendly advice," he growled, "next time you keep your sticky fingers to yourself if you don't want them bent out of shape."

Wyatt, however, was delighted by the threat, which testified to the other man's jangled nerves.

"Oh, you saw it too?" he whispered in awe, his voice cracking with fevered glee. "You're one of us then! You are—don't deny it! I felt that fabric that covers you and it's the same as mine! But that's just the outside... Place a hand on your belly and tell me you don't feel something there starting to quicken that makes the song all the more sweeter to your ears!"

As he raved on, grinning and growing red-faced with enthusiasm, Greg stared at him with a sort of loathing pity, then released him in the midst of his excited babbling and rose to leave.

"Wait!" cried Wyatt after him, this time wise enough not to push his luck by seizing the other man's hands or feet, "take me with you! I need to hear that song again."

"Song? More like a cry for help..." Greg almost remarked but held back as a thought occurred to him.

"I heard you used to work here," he said, turning back to Wyatt, "that you know your way around the building."

"You heard right," answered Wyatt, sitting tall.

"Is there a female ward here?"

Wyatt seemed a little surprised. "Why do you ask?"

"That singing you heard was coming through the vent. I was wondering whether they might be connected to another ward in the building."

"That depends on the room," said Wyatt, dragging a finger across his bottom lip in thoughtful amusement. "Why don't you take me there and I'll tell you..."

At this point, Nader rolled over in his bed and lay facing them with his eyes half-closed in a drowsy stupor. But when he noticed Wyatt sitting up and talking to Greg, he bolted up, asked Wyatt how he was doing, and in return received a reassuring pat on his shoulder for his concern.

"Never mind," said Greg, heading for the door. "You still have your friends here. Well, most of them."

"Clark's gone missing," Nader added to clarify.

"Is he now?" Wyatt paused to consider and moved his head slowly as if tracking an insect flying across the room. But the sound of the door interrupted his brief reverie, and again he called after Greg, who by then had left.

The staff's quarters were still deserted, still shrouded in a blackout. Greg found his way to the closest apartment and closed the bathroom door behind him. It was pitch black, but it was quiet and isolated, and the air was dry in there and less stifling than the shelter.

As he stripped down, he found his stomach slightly distended, more so to the right, and hesitantly pressed his fingers over it, probing for any dull ache, and also half-expecting to feel some movement there. Finding none, he gave a choked laugh of relief, and felt like an idiot for paying heed to Wyatt's ramblings.

Some minutes later, he stood before the dust-covered sink, absently letting the water run and gurgle down the sink hole while he squinted at the scar on his hand under the glare of his penlight. He had removed the surgical tape and gauze to wash his hands, and found the cut down his palm had closed and healed well, leaving a pink scar line, which he traced meditatively with his fingers. It bothered him. True, healing as promptly as it did was convenient, given the limited resources, but it bothered him nonetheless.

The water went on streaming down the sink, masking the creak of floorboards from the room outside, leaving Greg unaware that someone was on the other side until he heard a knock and profanely hissed as he shined the light on the door.

His clothes were laid over the edge of the tub, and he stole back towards them, intent on retrieving one of the knives, all the while keeping the light trained on the door, as though the glowing circle would seal the door against intruders. It occurred to him then that it would be smarter to try to barricade the door first, and he froze with sudden indecisiveness.

"Greg? Are you in there?" called a voice from the other side; it sounded familiar, but his panic-stricken mind could not put a name to it.

"He's in there," said another voice, this one thinner than the former. "The orderlies are still following protocol and keeping to the convalescent ward."

"It's just us," said the first voice—Nader's voice, Greg now remembered. The door handle began to move. "You okay in there?"

Greg shoved the door shut. "I'm fine. What do you want?"

"Sorry. I heard the faucet water running but when I didn't get an answer, I thought—"

"Give the guy a break," said Hitch, his voice farther behind but loud with exaggerated sympathy. "Maybe he just wanted to cover the noise while he laid a few bricks."

"Anyway, we'll just be out here when you're ready," said Nader.

When he emerged, Greg found them sitting in the dark room waiting for him.

"What brings you all here?" he asked, looking from one face to another. "I'm sure this isn't the only bathroom in the area…"

"Wyatt followed you here," said Nader. "We just came after him."

"You've been feeding him some cock-eyed story about singing sirens?" asked Hitch.

Greg drew his eyebrows together in confusion, but before he could say anything, Wyatt spoke up with: "The room with the singing voice."

"This again?" said Greg with exasperation. "Why don't you ask Hitch? I'm sure he knows the way."

Hitch, leaning against a wall with his arms crossed, gave a small shrug. "I don't know what you two are babbling about."

"You were in the same room when we heard it—that female singing voice."

"Oh, trust me, if I heard anything of the female persuasion, you think I'd have let it go by unnoticed?" laughed Hitch, his sullen expression giving in to a lascivious grin.

"He thinks it might be coming from a vent that connects to the ladies ward," added Wyatt to further stoke Hitch's interest, and the latter's eyes lit up at the revelation.

"There's a ladies ward?" he asked, then clicked his tongue admonishingly at Greg. "And here you thought you could skip out on us after we fed and sheltered you…"

"Wait a minute," Nader spoke up. "What about our escape plan?"

"Quiet, boy. Grown-ups are talking," said Hitch without taking his eyes off Greg, whose only reaction was an exasperated smile at the ridiculous turn the conversation took.

Wyatt had meanwhile placed his hand on Nader's shoulder. "I have a hunch we'll find Clark there as well."

"What!" cried Greg, before Nader turned on him: "I thought you said you looked everywhere!"

Greg gave an incredulous laugh. "He's making it up—he is! He's obviously saying what you all want to hear. Hitch was there and he didn't see anyone."

Hitch raised his hands, as though to relinquish himself of any responsibility. "Hey, I wasn't the one distracted enough to climb up the wall to sample some weird noise."

"Well, look whose memory just came back…" muttered Greg, lunging towards Hitch, who shrank back before Nader stepped in.

"Greg—Greg! Listen—" Nader said, pushing him back. "Let's just go there. It wouldn't hurt to look again. We're already here, what's a few doors down?"

On the face of it, there was nothing insulting in the suggestion, and yet it rankled Greg to have his testimony pushed aside in favor of Wyatt's alleged hunch. At the same time, he could not blame the boy for fostering the slightest hope in finding his friend—or his ticket to crossing the border, as it were. Besides, why did he hesitate when a short trip to an empty room was enough to vindicate him?

A few minutes later they stood in the doorway of the room, marked by the toppled chair and bed that was pushed against the wall. Only now the bed was occupied by a blond inmate, who slept peacefully with one hand folded over his chest.

CHAPTER 14

Nader stopped in his tracks and made a small movement to shrug Clark into a better position and keep him from slipping off his back. He did not think himself capable of carrying his tall friend but made a stalwart effort of it and was doing fine, so long as he stopped at regular intervals to shrug his friend into a more secure position. Clark's head rested on his left shoulder, and was now humming some tune close to Nader's ear. It was a low sound, discernible only when the whole group grew quiet, but to Nader, the proximity of the incessant, almost nasal hum grew more irritating, like the thin drone of a winged insect he was incapable of swatting away. Worse yet was how the humming was punctuated with small yet audible intakes of breath. He shrugged again hoping it would have the same effect as kicking a snoring bedfellow.

They were making their way in a line down a narrow corridor, following Wyatt's lead, and given that their path was more or less straightforward, Greg kept his flashlight off to save some battery. Either that or he could see better in the dark—at least he seemed capable of avoiding the large cobwebs, leaving Nader to flinch each time he brushed against one.

Speak of the devil, Nader found him waiting for them to catch up before offering to carry Clark on his back.

"No, I got it," said Nader, picking up the pace.

They walked on in silence, until Nader stopped to catch his breath and shift the weight to relieve his arms for a moment before they failed him.

Again, Greg waited for him with a renewed offer to carry Clark. Again, Nader demurred.

"I said I got it," he insisted with audible strain. "At least this way I know we won't accidentally lose him."

The tone of the remark stopped Greg in his tracks. "What's that supposed to mean?"

"You tell me," said Nader, his speech fluttering in his breathless state. "You said you couldn't find him—when there he was all along. But you left him—there—" he stopped to catch his breath. "Anyway—I'm fine."

Greg resumed his pace but spoke over his shoulder. "Not that your good opinion matters, kid, but I'm only going to say this once: that room was empty when we checked it. Hours had passed before we all went back to it. Your friend could have showed up there at any point in the interval."

This seemed to mollify Nader, until he spoke up again. "Then why'd you say—Wyatt was lying?"

"Because he was. He just made a lucky guess."

"Either way we'd have missed Clark if we hadn't—"

Greg yawned audibly. "Look, kid, what do you want from me? You're right—you win this argument, you win all future arguments. Alright? Just drop it."

"Ignore him," said Hitch, ahead of them. "Now that Clark's back, he wants nothing to do with any of us degenerates."

"Degenerates?" asked Greg, while Hitch went on: "I mean look at them: a martyr and a bleeding-heart—these two were made for each other. Only I can't stomach bleeding-hearts like him who pretend they care for others, and then watch what happens when some thug shows up waving a gun, and see if your good Samaritan doesn't grab the nearest warm body for a human shield. I know the type. I've seen—Why are we stopping?"

They stopped short of running into Wyatt, who pressed his hands against a wooden wall where a door was outlined with grey light radiating from the other side. "It's a dead end," he said.

"Where are we, anyway?" asked Greg, stifling another yawn.

Wyatt traced a few invisible lines against the door as he spoke, as though charting a map.

"This building used to be manor. Right now we're in one of the passages that connects the servants hall to the rest of the building. It was made for servants to travel discreetly about the manor—it's hidden, but not exactly a secret. They must have barricaded this one."

"Do they know we're here?" asked Hitch, then barked back at Nader to shut up with Clark's humming.

"If they suspected we were here, they'd have sent someone after us," said Wyatt. "No, it's more likely they're securing the area—perhaps they think the shooter is here, which explains why the place is deserted."

Greg gave the door a few shoves, as did Hitch, but even their combined effort proved futile.

"Let's go back," said Wyatt. "I'm sure there's a door they might have overlooked."

"Could we—take a short break first?" said Nader, squeezing the words out before his knees buckled and he dropped to a kneel.

"No breaks. We need to move now!" said Hitch, trying to drag Nader up by the arm; the boy remained anchored in his position, and almost fell over offloading Clark, who merrily went on humming the same maddening tune.

"I still have those pills," began Nader, catching his breath. "Maybe I could wake him up like I did with Wyatt."

"That'll take hours," Hitch protested. "Our window of opportunity is narrow enough as it is. I'm not going to wait around any longer."

"Then I'll stay," said Nader, sitting against the wall next to Clark. "You all go ahead if you want..."

There was an uncomfortable moment before Hitch spoke up: "Don't be stubborn, boy…" and Greg added: "We can take turns carrying him."

"Look, boy, I get it," Hitch went on. "You've tried your best, you carried him all the way here. But you have to face the fact that now it's either you or him. If you can't carry him anymore, drop him. No one's going to think less of you for it."

"The hell you care?" said Nader with a parched laugh. "You were satisfied to wait until Wyatt woke up. I guess he's of more use to you than Clark. Well, guess what? I'm tired of doing things your way and I'm not about to ditch my friend. You have your guide—just go already."

After a stretch of silence, Hitch spat on the floor, muttered:

"To hell with you," and left with the others following. Nader listened to their retreating footsteps as he bowed his head and leaned forward, clutching his knees and waiting for the hammering in his chest to die down. Eventually he stretched his legs out and sat back with a sigh, somewhere between resignation and relief.

"I guess it's just us now," he said, turning to where Clark sat without seeing much of anything. He reached for the folded paper tucked in his rolled-up sleeve, then paused when he realized Clark had stopped humming.

"Clark," he called into the darkness. "Clark?"

There was no answer. He unwrapped the paper in a hurry, and his hands, clumsy and trembling with fatigue, almost dropped the capsules. He caught them up, careful not to break their delicate shell. But the transient moment of relief soon evaporated when he realized Clark was no longer at his side. He blindly felt along the empty walls, and for a wild moment he was almost sure the group had stolen back and carried Clark away as a practical joke.

"You guys don't quit, do you!" he cried out, then listened for hints of stifled laughter.

Instead, a flare of light filled the narrow corridor. Or so it seemed to Nader as he squinted and held out his hand against it.

"Where's Clark?" he demanded, addressing the figure holding the flashlight and leaning against the wall—not with levity, but resting his head as though he was too tired to stand without something to prop him up. Instead of answering, Greg pointed the light at the dead-end door, where Clark stood with his back to them. His eyes were still closed when Nader turned him around, but he complied to be taken by the hand and guided to sit on the floor.

"At least he's quiet now," observed Greg, before giving in to another yawn.

"Thank God for that," said Nader.

Though he seemed to have walked off on his own, nothing they did roused Clark from his sleep, nor could they coax him to stand up again after Nader had laid him down to administer the capsule in the same manner he had done to Wyatt.

Now Greg bore Clark across his shoulders in a fireman's carry as they retraced their steps in search of an alternative route.

"You think we can catch up to them?" Nader asked.

"They can't be that far ahead," answered Greg, sweeping the penlight vigilantly for any diverging corridors.

They walked on in silence, then Nader spoke up. "Hey, listen—I just want to say thanks… for coming back."

"Yeah, well, maybe next time you'll be less mule-headed about asking for help," Greg muttered. "We didn't go through all that trouble looking for Clark just so you could play martyr."

"I know—I mean, you're right, I owe him that much at least."

Though his eyes were heavy with sleep, Greg turned a sharp glance at Nader—or tried to, anyway, since the body he carried obscured his view. "You don't owe him nothing. All he did was promise to take you across the border, and even that I'd take with a grain of salt if I were you."

"It's not just that," Nader rejoined. "See, I wasn't part of the group—at least not at first. When news first came about the shooting incident, we had to line up to be taken somewhere safe. I was near the end of the line, and the others—Clark, Wyatt, and Hitch—stood behind me. The orderly was counting heads starting at the end of the line. After he passed us by, I could see out of the corner of my eye the three of them breaking from the line and sneaking away. The orderly was still moving up the line, so I broke away and saw them disappear behind a corner. But when I turned that same corner, I found nothing but an empty hallway. That's when I felt a tap on my shoulder and turned around to find Clark peering out from behind a false panel in the wall. He signed me to stay quiet and follow him. Of course, Hitch raised hell when he saw me, saying three missing inmates was bad enough, but with four of us, they were sure to come after us. But Clark stood up for me and—"

The anecdote was cut short when Nader ran into Greg, who stood leaning against the wall. The small jolt caused the penlight to fall from his slackened hand.

Nader stooped to pick it up before focusing it on the other's face.

"How did you—" he stammered on finding Greg asleep. "Hey, wake up!"

Greg jerked his head back and gave it a shake, surfacing from a dream in which he was trekking back to a riverside camp under a late autumn sky smote with gold, carrying a freshly killed deer that was still warm against his shoulders.

"You were asleep," said Nader.

"I wasn't. I just closed my eyes for a second—Hey!" he languidly protested as Nader felt his forehead. "Your hands are cold."

"I think you have a fever," said Nader, focusing the light on Greg's mouth. "Here—open your mouth."

"Why?"

"I'm checking for other symptoms. You might be coming down with something. Stick out your tongue and say 'ah.'"

"Get out of my face. We're not playing doctor."

"Greg, come on. We need to know what to look out for."

"Alright, fine. But if you say I have Yang deficiency or menstrual problems, I'll slap you."

"Hmm," murmured Nader, "everything seems normal. Your tonsils aren't swollen either."

"I'm fine," insisted Greg. "Just caffeine-deprived. Must've—minute there," he slurred before his eyes began to close again.

"Oh, no, not you too," groaned Nader, shaking Greg's shoulders. "Good God—you're like a horse the way you sleep on your feet. Come on, wake up! We're all screwed if you don't wake up. You know I can barely carry Clark, let alone the two of you."

He went on, talking and patting Greg's face until it furrowed into a severe expression and he gave a crotchety growl.

"Whatever it is, you're definitely coming down with it—just like Wyatt and Clark. Maybe I'm immune because I took a capsule earlier. I still have one left." He fished in his sleeve for the last capsule. "Here—take it before you get any worse."

The red capsule was suddenly in Greg's hand. He opened his eyes to find he was somehow still on his feet, with Clark somehow still on his shoulders. Then sleep pulled him down, yearning in its honeyed grasp. His eyelids drooped, as did the half-closed hand that held the capsule, until Nader pushed it back up to prompt Greg to take it.

Irritated, Greg wrested his hand free, muttered some slurred threat, then lifted his hand and swallowed the capsule himself.

In a green-tiled room, Dr. Carver peeled off his gore-painted surgical gloves, and took a moment to regard his patient, not quite dead yet, but laid open on the surgery table like a body in the midst of an autopsy. Remnants of a dreamy smile creased the corners of the patient's mouth, and now and then his eyelids fluttered under the influence of a vision that was slowly sinking to black.

"This is it," sighed Carver, "I've done all I could now."

He took off the surgical mask, which seemed redundant now, as any previous time when he was preparing the body for disposal. But then he supposed old habits die hard.

After washing his hands, Carver slid a tape into the cassette player and hummed along to the old sentimental song, switching the lights off before leaving the room.

The tape kept rolling, a lone voice lamenting against a chorus as it echoed across the dim and deserted room.

Soon came a thudding and skidding sound of something dragging itself through the air vents. And from the mouth of the open duct came a thin spray of dust that spilled over the patient.

CHAPTER 15

Behind his closed mouth, Greg scraped his tongue along the edge of his teeth, testing their sharpness and tasting the familiar traces of the capsule. Whatever its purpose, the capsule had breathed fire into him, and his heart smoldered pleasantly through the low-key rush. Even the weight on his shoulders felt more agreeable than encumbering. He walked with a sober gait, though his legs were nervous with stored energy, and he felt that if he were to break into a run, he could bound as effortlessly as an astronaut on the moon, even while shouldering an unconscious man. Everything seemed possible then: within the hour they would find their way out, find some means of navigating through the glass-littered grounds with minimal injury, and finally make it to his compact pick-up truck, which he had parked somewhere down the mountain path, sheltered from sight and sun under the low branches of a viridian thicket.

Cars were one's lesser home, little more than transportation and transient offices. And yet the slam of the car door is often followed by a relieved sigh, however small and imperceptible, of one finding shelter; few ever sigh like that after closing their home's front door—in his mind, at least. Homes, even apartments, were too big, with the possibility of something lurking in any one of the many rooms; behind the shower curtain and closet doors—or so he'd often tell himself. But a car has little space to hide trespassers; and if the neighborhood was not safe, he could simply drive off to a better place, often to any one of the several spots he memorized in several towns, cities, and counties where he could park inconspicuously and sleep without being disturbed. And the car, not living yet alive, humming good-naturedly over concrete roads and grazing the gravel paths, and then cradling him while he dozed in the front seat or slept in the back. Sometimes he caught himself regarding his truck with something like tenderness and awe, as if he'd won the lottery with this hardy model that had stayed with him for the past ten years, held his life together, and asked for little more than gas and the occasional maintenance work to keep going.

"Any of your relatives live nearby?" Nader asked out of the blue, landing Greg back in the narrow corridor.

"Why? Looking to crash somewhere?"

"No, I was just wondering."

Greg considered the question. "You know, I've been living on my own for so long it never occurred to me to look them up."

"On your own? No friends or family?"

"Got a network of friendly acquaintances, if that's what you mean."

"No—I mean, where do you go for the holidays?"

"Wherever I please."

"But doesn't it get lonely?"

"What are you, my mother? I'm happy with my life. Between living on my own and getting tied down, I'd rather live by my standards. I happen to like solitude—I don't bother anyone, and no one bothers me. Besides, there's a world of difference between loneliness and being alone: the first you can experience in a room full of people; the second is the status quo—the sooner you learn to make peace with it, the less likely you'll fall apart when others decide to break things off and move on."

Nader hesitated. "Did that ever happen? Someone left you to move on?"

Greg gave a soft chuckle meant to dismiss the solemnity of the subject. "Happens to everyone at some point, I'm sure."

They found a small door that opened into a cylindrical stairwell with a set of concrete stairs spiraling upwards, dimly lit by narrow windows through which rain drizzled, slicking some of the steps. On the whole, it looked very different from the stairwell Greg had traveled through to reach the lobby.

"You sure these won't just take us up to the roof or something?" Nader asked as Greg began to mount the stairs in slow, heavy steps.

"We'll just have to go up and see," said Greg before biting down on the penlight to free his hand and steady himself on the brick wall. They did not go far before the effort of climbing the steps while carrying Clark grew formidable, and Nader had to position himself behind Greg, half-supporting, half-pushing him up the stairs.

The door at the top opened into a dark and dilapidated hallway, where sheets of tarp hung like giant cobwebs, and the walls were pocked with mold under the peeling paint. Wind whistled down the corridor, billowing the tarp and filling the air with a chorus of low, unrelenting moans.

Greg lingered in the relative safety of the doorway, breathing heavily and feeling lightheaded after the climb.

"Maybe we can—access the main stairwell from here," he said, as if pausing to consider the path ahead, though in truth he wanted a moment to allow the dizziness to subside.

They let the penlight cut through the dark ahead of them, moving with slow, deliberate steps, toes bent back before each foot landed in front of the other to minimize contact with the debris and glass-littered floor.

Nader stuck close to Greg. "At least we're not likely to run into any orderlies in this hole," he murmured.

Doesn't mean we're alone here, thought Greg. As with the orderly's apartment, he was plagued by the feeling of something tracking their movement: a pair of eyes watching them from the dark, or perhaps—he lifted the light to the sagging ceiling above—hidden cameras? He both wanted to put the question to rest, and at the same time was afraid to answer it.

Then came a single sob, reverberating from deep down the hallway, beyond the penlight's reach. He stopped cold and held his breath, waiting for the sob to repeat itself, almost jumping out of his skin when Nader bumped into him. It still echoed in his mind, shrill, floating like a wisp of smoke that curled onto itself and disappeared; yet nothing followed it in the profound silence.

"Hey, Greg—"

"Not now," hissed the other, resuming his slow pace, feet weighed down with hesitation, eyes sharp and wide open, darting to catch sight of shadows that leapt out of sight the moment he looked their way. He closed his mouth and scraped his tongue against his teeth, listening to the dull grinding sound it made in his head, trying hard to stay focused, trying hard not to misstep and fall on his face; it was challenging enough with the dead weight on his shoulders, but even the once steady floor now seemed to rush up towards him every time he looked down, or tipped and tilted underfoot like the deck of a storm-tossed ship.

"Listen," said Nader. "We can move faster if we both carry Clark. I'll take the arms and you take the legs..."

"And who's going to hold the flashlight then?" said Greg, before whipping his head towards a wall where a tall figure stood—but, no, it was nothing more than a long, dark splatter on the wall. "Besides," he went on, "it's hard enough to see where we're going without one of us walking backwards in the dark." His stomach turned at the idea of walking backwards.

"But, Greg, you don't look good..."

"And you're no prize yourself..."

"No, I mean you walk funny."

"So will you if you don't shut up."

Nader gave an exasperated sigh, then pointed to one of the rooms. "Look, I think I see a table there. How about we lay Clark there while we take a breather?"

The large table was piled with cardboard boxes, which they pushed aside to make room for Clark. One of the smaller boxes fell to Greg's feet, spilling out cassette tapes in a plastic clatter.

Nader helped take Clark off his shoulders, and the sudden lightness brought on a new wave of vertigo that almost felled Greg had he not grabbed the table's edge.

"Something's not right," he growled apprehensively, leaning his elbows against the table and clutching his head. "It's like I'm trapped in one of those spinning rides."

"You still have those dog treats on you?" asked Nader after a thoughtful pause.

"Only if you sit up and beg," said the other through a pained groan.

"I meant for you. Maybe your blood pressure dropped—could be a side-effect or something."

"I thought you said no side-effects."

"*I* didn't experience any, and neither did Wyatt—I think. But there's always a small chance… Anyhow, see if you can eat something. I'll go see if I can find a gurney or a wheelchair or something we can use for Clark."

"Wait," said Greg, pulling one of the knives out and offering it to Nader. "Take this. I can't shake the feeling we're not alone here." And seeing Nader's face cloud with doubt, he went on: "Just take it. If you can't find anything, use it to cut down the tarp—a large piece, about six feet in length. We'll use it to drag Clark."

Nader took the knife, then faltered. "I could use a flashlight…"

And after a moment's hesitation, Greg extended the penlight, but held it out of reach before Nader could take it.

"At the least sign of trouble, you come back, you hear? Don't make me come after you."

Nader gave a solemn nod, and Greg watched the light

disappear with Nader as he left, then carefully lowered himself and sat on the floor.

Silence and darkness settled over him. He no longer felt someone was watching him, but there was little relief in that: after all, there's a world of difference between the absence of danger and being insensible to its presence. A small sound made him jump, and only after he realized it was Clark murmuring in his sleep did Greg berate himself for going to pieces.

As he settled back, his hand fell on one of the cassette tapes littering the floor from the overturned box. He picked it up and traced his fingers on its surface, as though they would somehow decipher the label. At any rate it could keep him distracted until Nader returned, and ejecting his own tape from the recorder, he slid in this new one, and pressed play.

The tape turned out to be an amateur recording of a man narrating a story in a bright, paternal voice, all tobacco smoke and molasses. All the same, Greg let the tape roll, listening while he reached for the bag of jerky to address his dizziness.

"Once there was a child, who wandered into the forest and got lost. Seized with apprehension, the child ran in every direction trying to find the way home. Soon the child grew tired and thirsty, and went to look for a river. But no river was to be found in the dark, sleepy forest. The desolate child began to weep when, suddenly, a kind-faced fairy appeared, and offered the child a drink from a cup. The child drank and drank from the cup, drank something that was not water but was nevertheless cold and refreshing and made the child forget. When the cup was drained, the child looked up at the kind-faced fairy and smiled—smiled with happiness because nothing troubled the child anymore.

'What is your name?' asked the fairy.

'I don't know,' said the child.

'Where did you come from?' asked the fairy.

'I don't know,' said the child.

'Have you a mother? Have you a father?' asked the fairy.

'I don't know,' said the child.

Hand in hand, the fairy and the child walked into the forest until they disappeared out of sight."

There was a brief pause, but just when the narrator was about to resume, his voice was cut off by a click of someone recording over the original audio.

"Carver's up to something. He briefed us today about a new scheme of his—said he wants to allow a few inmates to wander around the building looking for a way out, and we're supposed to turn a blind eye to them—unless, of course, they really are close to escaping, or they saw us looking for them and we have to drop the pretense and go after them. In other words, he wants to release them into the building like mice in a maze, and we're supposed to play our part and let them have that false hope of escape before going in after them. Sounds crazier now that I've said it. The orderlies seem to like the idea of playing cat-and-mouse with the inmates. Carver says the scheme works like a release valve: the whole point is for them to have this false hope of escape to keep them from going nuts like they do from time to time. But he can't be this careless, not when we've had inmates disappearing. I mean, sure, they were found later, but the state they were in—Shit! I have to cut it short. Watch yourself."

The recording ended here and the story resumed. It took Greg a few seconds to take in what he heard before he rewound the tape to listen to the recorded message again. It was the same voice, or rather the same man who had left him the recorded message. And yet Nader had attributed the voice to the nameless inmate he met in the apartments, whereas this one mentioned being briefed, indicating he was one of the staff—or perhaps used to be, Greg amended, remembering Wyatt's situation.

He fast-forwarded and played the tape at intervals to check for more messages. There were none, so he ejected the cassette, picked up another to listen to, and almost dropped the device when he heard himself talking on tape—or rather, heard a voice identical to his own.

"—sleep better at night thinking the government and its departments all fall under one head. But that's far from true. Ever heard of a medical condition called Alien hand syndrome? Those who have it experience a strange phenomenon in which their hands behave as if they have a mind of their own. It usually occurs in cases where a person has had the two hemispheres of their brain surgically separated. You could say the same applies to certain arms of the government; but such branches—or arms, if you like—are well-hidden from plain view, operating covertly and leaving no paper trail behind. I know this doesn't answer your question, but that's all I'm willing to say about the matter."

The audio log stopped, and then a new one began.

"You better watch how you replace the device. After my 'therapy' session, Carver walked me back to my cell, and as soon as I walked in, I noticed the recorder almost poking out from under the mattress. I had to sit on the edge of the bed to cover it with my legs. If Carver had suspected anything, he'd have had the cell turned inside out by now, though I can't be sure whether or not he noticed something and pretended not to. Just to be safe, kemosabe, I'll hold off answering your questions until I'm sure."

Another entry followed.

"By your count a week had passed already. Has it? It's hard for me to say without something to help me keep track—a clock, a watch, a sundial even! I know how to keep track of time without a timepiece, but I find it hard to focus these days, thanks to my sleeping schedule—you know the meds haven't made it any easier: I roll and toss like I'm on a bed of hot coals, though my hands and feet are freezing. And when I fall asleep, I jump awake all panicked, like I've been falling down a long well. Carver doesn't seem to know, which is reassuring, but I can't be sure—I can't be sure. I can't even record this without stopping to look under the door and listen for footsteps, though God knows how men that size manage to pad every sound; their joints don't crack and their footsteps are silent. How do you do it, kemosabe? How do you keep from making so much noise when you move? Answer me this, please. But first I have to answer your question, don't I? I have to tell you what I promised to answer while my head is still clear. They're hard to kill, but that's not the worst of it. They'll eat corpses but that's not why they hunt; if they attack, they don't go for the kill, they go for the limbs. You don't need your limbs to stay alive, which they need you to be: you've more use to them alive than dead. And that's how they want to keep you. So if the— if the— (What's the word I'm looking for?) If the needle misses its mark, or the neurotoxin doesn't work, they will instead try to break your limbs before they drag you away... To be honest, I don't know what's worse, and I imagine the neurotoxin doesn't exactly put you to sleep as much as act on the neuromuscular junction to inhibit signaling and induce muscle relaxation—that is to say you're awake but can't move or do anything about it. Anyway, I don't imagine that's worse than being dragged away with all your bones broken, screaming in agony, which is something I've only heard from afar but never experienced, small mercy. Where was I going with this? I know I wanted to say something more—it keeps buzzing around my head just beyond my reach – but my mind's drawing a blank. I better end it here. If I remember something, I'll add it later."

The next entry was preceded a long spell of silence.

"What day is it? The only thing I remember are the five witnesses that saw the secret ceremony in the yard. That's how it was until it wasn't. But the relentless song haunts me still like the fevered incantations of bog creatures. Samson talked about it before he left; you know how it gets. Nothing that a few drops in each eye won't help. I'm fine now, but I lost control then."

The following and final entry appeared to have been recorded covertly; the voices sounded faded and distant and were over-imposed with the noise of fabric rubbing against the microphone. Yet it was clear that the distant voice belonged to Carver.

"There's n——voiding the procedure. ——want the—peration with anesthesia? I want——"

A stretch of silence followed; and then: "—Very well," before the recording stopped.

CHAPTER 16

Someone was in the house. The boy started awake and listened through the brief silence until he heard the muffled and distant slam of the front door. He threw off the blanket and stood close to the locked closet door, expecting to hear his twin bounding up the stairs.

But instead, he heard the mumbling voices of men talking downstairs.

Daylight seeped into the closet from under the door. The whole night had passed without anyone returning to relieve him of his confinement. And now there were strangers in the house.

Faint with hunger, the boy almost slammed his fists on the door and called out to them, but in a moment of clarity remembered what the father had hammered into his and his twin's head. Should a stranger ever enter the house, he or his twin was not to make any noise that would reveal their presence to trespassers.

Better they rob the house than take you away, the father had explained.

This was compounded by repeated warnings against talking to anyone besides the teachers whenever one or the other attended school. And if the boys had a vague idea of what the father was warning them against, posters at school on Stranger Danger filled in the gaps.

The father himself seemed always wary of someone following them whenever they left the house, and the boy usually caught him looking over his shoulder, if not scanning the area and checking for an unnamed threat that never appeared. Likewise, the boy also observed the mother's exasperated expression whenever the father failed to run errands or returned home late because, as he would say, someone looked at him in a suspicious way, or he took a different route trying to lose a car that was tailing him. Parents might think their children are too self-absorbed to notice anything, but when tension is ever-present in the house, children often develop internal barometers and can read the air, understanding by instinct the things they can't put into words. If the mother never said anything in front of the boys, her look said enough: she was tired of living like this.

But now—and this was a first—these two strangers coming up the stairs, their voices growing louder with their proximity, they vindicated the father's apprehensions and filled the boy with unprecedented terror. They were coming for him.

If they opened the closet, searching for something—or searching for him—that would be it.

He backed away from the door, slipped behind a curtain of long winter coats that hung in the closet, and stood on tiptoes, pressing himself into a corner. He squeezed his eyes shut and listened but did not catch what they said; his panicked mind was full of white noise.

Then it grew quiet. The boy opened his eyes and listened to any signs of movement or retreat. Were they gone? He opened his eyes, peered out from behind the coats, and found the line of daylight that seeped under the closet door had been effaced by a shadow of someone standing on the other side.

Greg faltered in the pitch dark hallway and called out to Nader. Any qualms he had about keeping quiet and remaining hidden from the unseen presence that followed him was pointless when, thanks to his improvised footwear, his tapping footsteps already gave away his position.

The tapes he heard had all but lit a fire under him, driving him to rush out in search of Nader, only to be impeded after stepping on glass fragments or something equally small and sharp—something he might have sidestepped had he the penlight to see where it was safe to tread. He still had some leftover surgical tape, and after he had brushed away the pieces that stuck to the soles of his feet and checked for any signs of bleeding, he considered using the tape he had to cover them, when another idea occurred to him, and he went back for one of the cardboard boxes, tore off the flaps, pared them down, and bound them to his feet with the surgical tape. The cardboard sole served to protect his feet while the tape covering it provided traction. Satisfied with the result, he repeated the process with the other foot.

Presently he walked with one hand holding the knife and the

other skimming over the tarp-covered walls for guidance. He didn't like touching the tarp, not when there were faces within the folds, and they turned to face him whenever they felt his touch.

"Nader," he called, and waited for the echoes to die out.

He turned a corner and was about to call again when he heard something tapping, and stopped. The taps came again from a near distance. He approached them and reluctantly felt along the walls until his hands fell on the smooth slab of a door. Behind it came the sharp tapping, and he leaned against the door to listen. It sounded close to his ear that he could almost see the fingernail tapping on the other end. He tapped the knife against the door in answer.

The tapping from the other side stopped at the unexpected report, then tapped a different rhythm. Greg knew the code and understood.

"They hear you," said the taps.

"Who hears me?" he tapped in return

"They bad," said the taps.

"Are you safe in there?"

"I want out but I don't want they to find me."

"Nobody's here."

"They is here."

"Do you have enough to eat in there?" he tapped.

There was no tapping in return. All the same, he took out the bag of jerky, taped it to the door, and left.

Some distance later, he pressed the heels of his hands against his brow, against the persistent headache that pounded there. He began to feel stifled, and sneered and pulled at the collar of the Skins which seemed to choke his throat. Under his clasping fingers, he felt the suit suddenly bulk and inflate, gaining inches of dense mass, compressing his body in the process. It pressed over the tender spot in his right side, and the effect was like receiving a kick to his kidney. His vision burst into stars. Pain bolted up through his right side, weakening his legs; with a cry he fell to his hands and knees. The pressure did not relent, as if the entire suit had suddenly shrunk a few sizes. He was forced to ignore the pain and wrest his arms out of the coveralls sleeves to reach the Skins' zipper. But when he tried to pull the slider, he found it stuck fast and went back to pulling the collar to keep it from strangling his throat; it held close, almost adhering to it, and try as he would, he might as well have tried to peel off his own skin.

Then the pressure began to subside, allowing his chest to rise with the first generous intake of air before it was wracked with coughs. As they died down, he tried hooking his fingers into the collar and relieve his burning throat. Far from being light and supple, the Skins now was dense with raised slabs like armor plates, which nonetheless projected under the fabric instead of materializing over it. And while he was able to breathe well enough, his movement was now less free, and he had the impression he was somehow hermetically sealed within it. How and what triggered it was beyond his understanding. Again he patted his left shoulder, feeling for the zipper, and his bloodshot eyes grew wide when he realized he couldn't find it—or rather felt it buried under a layer of the Skins' own leathery fabric.

He took his knife and hesitated a moment before pointing it towards the back of his wrist, hoping to slip it into the sleeve and pry it away, or perhaps undo the vacuum-like seal by letting some air in. At least that was his theory. But the sleeve held on as if it had been glued there, and after biting through a few agonizing moments while he tried to push the blade in and ungraft Skins from skin, it was soon evident the procedure would do more harm than good; he swore and flung the knife away in frustration.

His right side radiated a dull ache of which he was aware but paid no heed.

There were times when he felt the world close in on him, but never like this; all past troubles and worries melted under the present cataract. He pressed the back of his hand to his mouth, the corners of which tensed as though he choked back something acerbic. No one was around him, but he swallowed his emotions all the same. If he were to collapse now, he feared he would lose something with it—perhaps self-respect or some illusion of being in control. He could not afford it, could not afford to think of himself as a hapless victim, even if it meant holding himself accountable for his decisions.

So be it, then: if circumstances walled up behind him, shutting him in with unforeseen consequences, there was nothing left but to move ahead and try to dig his way out—it didn't grant him any comfort, but then, neither did wallowing in remorse and self-pity. He exhaled sharply, venting some of his frustration, and lifted his chin as he rose to his feet in a show of resolve for his own benefit. The coveralls were half-removed, and not bothering to push his arms back into the sleeves, he tied them around his waist and went searching for his knife.

Some time later, after rounding a bend in the hallway, Greg discerned a weak white gleam radiating from one of the rooms, and gave a sigh of relief at having found Nader. The gleam did turn out to be the penlight, but it was left abandoned on the floor in the center of the room.

"Nader?" called Greg, looking about before stooping to pick up the penlight and survey the room with it. An old desk, a toppled chair, and a cabinet with broken glass panels occupied one corner of the room. As he approached the desk, something fell and crashed onto it, almost upsetting the penlight out of his hand.

It was the grille cover of the ceiling vent.

Greg shined the light up at the ceiling, searching for anything that might have caused the damage. All he saw were thin showers of dust and soot, shimmering briefly in the glow of the penlight as they cascaded from the gaping vent.

Again he called for Nader, wondering if the boy had climbed into the vent. But a moment later he realized his mistake when a croaky mimic of his voice answered his call, followed by a series of dull thumps and skids issuing from the vent.

He didn't wait to see what was coming but ducked under the desk, and it wasn't two seconds before he felt the desk shudder when something heavy landed on top of it. Whatever it was, it brought with it the sickening odor of moist earth and raw meat, and its mass slithered and seemed to pour itself down the sides of the desk.

Greg promptly extinguished the penlight and pressed his back to a corner of the confined space, trying to draw his knees close to his chest, though they remained hindered by the Skins' ossified state.

"Nader?" croaked the creature, hoping to draw out the call's originator. It kept its post over the desk, slithering its restless arms across the floor and chair before him, making a scraping noise as they pushed past it. One of them brushed over his bandaged foot, swept back and snaked over it again, twisting inquisitively, as though to get a better feel of what it found. He dissociated himself from his foot, trying to keep it as still as possible while he drew back the knife. But by the time he had it poised to strike, the prehensile limb had lost interest and slipped away.

Alarmed as he was, the confined space instilled a form of physical resignation that mitigated his panic: like a room full of tripwires, he had to work his way out with slow deliberation. But when a wave of the stench hit him, and he had to bury his face in the crook of his arm to suppress the brimming coughs, the desk creaked as the creature shifted its weight and began to poke into the desk drawer, and then probe under it with staccato taps, inches away from Greg's face.

He tilted his head back and held his breath, keeping the knife at the ready as he pulled out his handheld recorder, a finger poised on the play button, and set it quietly on the floor. The instant he pressed the play button, he shoved it away, sending it sliding from under the desk towards the other end of the room.

The creature almost toppled the desk over as it launched itself after the device, granting Greg some leeway to slip out from under the desk.

So far so good, he thought, stealing towards the door. That is, until the penlight, not properly tucked in its pocket, slipped and fell to the floor with a sharp tap and a wink of light.

He froze, and then realized the volume on the device had been turned up all the way, which might have covered the incidental sound. But as he turned to leave, something struck his feet with a violent sweep and felled him to the floor.

He raised his head with a pained groan, disoriented enough to believe he was sprawled facedown on the ceiling. His left eye stung from the blood streaming over it, and he felt something coiled around his leg and the floor slipping under him.

Somewhere in the room, the handheld recorder was still playing the tape: "No one has been here. That's blood crying in your ears..." but the creature had lost interest in favor of this thing it had in its grasp and was slowly reeling him in.

He wanted to repeat the same trick of throwing something to distract the creature, but had nothing on him. He considered planting his knife into the floor, but it was too smooth for that. And as he felt another tentacle coiling around his other leg, he knew he was fresh out of options.

He pushed against the floor, rolling onto his back, and began slashing blindly; though he felt the creature was near—the stench was stronger, and the cloud of humidity it gave off clung closer than sweat to his skin—the knife only cut through empty air.

One of his legs was raised, and Greg felt it caught between jaws that clamped hard on it. The Skins' plates preserved most of his leg against the pressure, but something like a piece of broken glass stabbed his foot and he screamed in agony.

He planted his hands on the floor and tried to drag himself away, but the creature descended over him like an avalanche and pinned him down. He found its flank and stuck his knife into it, gouging it over and over, but neither blood nor any vital liquid poured out of its thick hide; moreover, his attacks didn't seem to bother the creature in the least. It now tried to break his leg by bending it backwards at the knee, and at that same instant, in his effort to push away the huge mass that had settled over him, Greg's hand fell on a wet spongy aperture—an eye or breathing hole or even the corner of its mouth—at least he hoped it was any one of them. Nevertheless, he pushed his fingers into it without hesitation, and held on, maintaining a hooked grip, even as he felt it constrict and close around his fingers, even as the creature sounded a shrill cry and tried to twist itself free. He then plunged the blade in the same spot, almost slicing his fingers in his vehemence. It shrieked again and pulled away with a sudden violence that yanked the knife from his hand as it twisted away and fled.

CHAPTER 17

The closet door was ajar when he opened his eyes to the evening's red sun.

His family was having dinner in the kitchen downstairs.

He descended the stairs and passed them by, uninterested in joining them.

The strangers were still there, somewhere within the walls of the house.

He made his way to the living room as if set on a course from which he could not derail himself. There he found a table upon which sat a fruit bowl of fish, alive and gulping for air, with dilated pupils and black spots flickering on their scales as they died. One began to flop violently and threw itself at him.

Startled, the boy woke up to his dark cell.

Behind the beam of his penlight, Greg hobbled, stepping on one foot and then the heel of the other to keep the injury elevated, bound in cloth torn from the coveralls. Every other step brought fresh pain, but he pushed on, holding the tape recorder close to his mouth, whispering vehemently into it.

"Did you believe those stories, Greg? Do you still believe them?"

"Why would he lie to us?"

"I never said he lied. I asked if you believed those stories like he believed them. There's a difference."

He pressed the stop button to end the recording though he had never pressed the record button to start with.

Notions flickered in the back of his mind like dying embers: he should be looking for Nader; he should return to Clark. There was a vague feeling he was doing one or the other, but he wasn't sure. He tried to find his way back to Clark; in these labyrinthine corridors he felt like a fly trying to find its way out of an open bottle.

"All these rooms look sane to me," he said into the recorder, and tasting blood on his lips, put away the device and pressed another rag torn from the coveralls to his nose, which had begun hemorrhaging sometime after his encounter; along with the weeping cut over his left eye, half of his face was now streaked with blood. He wanted to rest, for time to suspend and his blood to clot, but kept moving for fear of falling asleep while the creature was still at large in the area. Perhaps luck was on his side that last time, but without a knife, he wasn't sure he could survive another encounter. The Skins had protected his legs, but if it were his head that those jaws had caught—

The thought amplified the persistent bite of his injury. As

a compromise, he stopped and lowered himself to the floor, resting his back against the wall. He pulled out the tape recorder, this time with the intention of listening to something to help him stay awake while he rested a moment. He spat the trace of blood that trickled into his mouth while he switched tape sides, then lowered the volume, held the device close to his ear, and listened. As with the previous logs, the same voice narrated the following entries.

"—can't imagine what it's like for the rest of them. I know I'll get out of here at some point, but being confined here is already taking its toll on me. Or perhaps the madness here is contagious. And that's just the healthy prisoners who didn't regress to eating their hair or smearing on the walls with their filth yet. They're not far, though—howling, kicking, and banging their heads and fists against the doors, and raising all kinds of hell just to break the routine and pay the heavy price for it. When I first came, the whole block used to get riled up over the entertainment. Now it's somewhat quieter after six or seven of them went missing. I think you know where I'm going with this, kemosabe. If we're going to do this, we need to be transparent with each other. Don't keep me in the dark."

"Alright, kemosabe: a warning next time would be great before you drag me to the penance room and strap in the chair for some story time. You nearly gave me a heart attack with that stunt, and I didn't know what the hell was going on until your voice came in. If we're going to do it this way, fine. Just don't get clumsy and leave those tapes lying around for others to hear. So, Carver's planning to let some poor bastards roam free… I have a feeling there's more to it than trying to break them with false hope. When do the orderlies know when to step in? And where do they end up once they're caught? Don't leave me hanging for an answer."

"Those orange armbands must mean something. I've only seen one or two inmates tagged with an orange armband, and even I can tell they're harmless at that point. No wonder Carver allows the nurses to tend to them. Though I wonder what would happen if they took one of those capsules I gave you... If you have access to the convalescent ward, I want you to try giving it to them. Don't go too crazy with it—say a capsule a day for each inmate to start with. It's not supposed to be administered in their cases, but I want to see what happens—that is, I want a report on it."

"Any other symptoms besides nosebleeding? What stage were they at? Did any of them get worse or better? If nothing happens, try increasing the dose if possible—but not too much. We wouldn't want them to overdose, and more importantly, I still need some for myself."

"How many capsules had you given him? Did he have a history of violence—before he got tagged, I mean? See if you could find it in his file. At least you were there to stop him. Hope the nurse thanked you for saving her. In the meantime, I can only imagine the incident will rouse Carver's suspicion, so hold back for now."

"I'm surprised you'd ask, given that you see it firsthand. But if you're only allowed in the ward a few minutes at a time, I guess it's not enough to give you a clear picture. From what I know, stage one is lethargy, followed by narcolepsy or hypersomnia. But I'm guessing you're asking more about stage two. If they shave their heads, it's to hide the hair loss, which they won't object to—they're too docile to object to anything. Their shaved heads, the progressive weight gain, and that meditative look and a small strange smile, as if they've transcended this world and achieved enlightenment—at least that's how one medic described it. There's something unnerving about them, and I've only seen photos of their cases. Think Lotus-eaters, if you've ever heard of them. They're capable of carrying a limited conversation if prompted, but they have no concept of time passing, and in effect, their memories are muddled together. They're happy just to be—there's no urge to get up and do anything except to eat and sleep. In other words, it's the kind of lifestyle that becomes you, Greg. Thirty years plus, and where are you now? But you weren't made to go out there and seize life by the hands. You're nothing more than the afterbirth that—"

Greg stopped the tape and pressed a hand to his side, unable to ignore the pain shooting up his side and lower back; it made him restless and goaded him into rising to his feet. He leaned against the wall for a moment, awash with sweat yet hoping in some confused way to find relief by moving. Again he was reminded of how much it hurt to walk, but kept moving to let the flank pain slide—slide and subside, that was the secret, as long as he kept moving, as long as he ignored it and limped on and allowed gravity to push it down…

Slide and subside, his mind echoed, a maddening chant looping in his head.

A wheelchair sat at the end of the corridor, waiting for him, and he all but collapsed with exhaustion into it, sending it drifting back a few feet. The brief motion was oddly calming, and he closed his eyes as he sank into it. The ache from his side persisted, and he shifted his weight, looking for some relief, however small. It was all he could do to manage the pain besides riding it out. But there was comfort in the motion of the chair as it rolled forward without his prompt or push.

He opened his eyes and lifted his head.

Though he couldn't see, he understood why the wheelchair was moving. It was strange—but the middle-aged nurse was behind him, pushing the wheelchair. She posed no direct threat, and her presence had the vague promise of medical attention; so he closed his eyes, resigned to be wheeled to wherever she chose to take him.

Then he remembered Nader and Clark, both unaccounted for, and wanted to turn to the nurse to tell her about it. But something constrained his movement, and in an instant he realized his hands and legs were bound to the chair by leather straps, and a broader strap was lashed over his chest and arms.

His eyes rolled up and back as he strained to look behind him but could only glimpse the bony knuckles of the nurse's hands.

"Wait—you don't need to do that," he stammered while she continued to wheel him.

She docked the chair with a metal clank, and he heard a long, authoritative "Shhh!" coming from behind before a helmet-like apparatus was lowered over his head, covering his eyes. He wrenched and threw his weight to one side, rattling the chair as it remained anchored to the floor. Then he heard the mechanical creak–slam of a large lever, followed by a rising thrum that overwhelmed him, until his overheated head went up in a mushroom cloud.

White heat faded into black. The walls of the crawlspace scraped hard against his shoulders. He kept moving with a series of vermicular motions, placing one forearm in front of the other to pull ahead, then lifting his hips and digging his toes into the floor to push forward. Light winked at the end of the tunnel, glowing quietly from a small lightbulb like a distant star. As he crawled towards it, it waxed larger and brighter, as if it, too, traveled towards him. Soon he was close enough to almost touch it. But as he reached out, the light went out, and in its brief dying glow, he glimpsed his own startled face staring back at him before the floor gave away and he plunged below.

He came to with a harsh gasp, his startled eyes casting about the recesses of the room before he sat bolt upright.

The penlight, left glowing on the floor, drew his attention, and looking there, he found Nader sprawled facedown on the floor.

"Nader?" called Greg, crouching beside him, wanting to turn him over yet afraid to move him without knowing the nature of his injury: as he checked Nader's pulse, he caught the dank smell of urine, which alone was a bad sign. Then, after an anxious survey during which he clenched and unclenched his hands in a spell of hesitation, he called Nader a few times and patted his cheek until the latter's eyelids fluttered and he made a thin, weak sound.

"It's okay, I'm here," Greg reassured him. "Can you move?"

Nader's brow furrowed over his closed eyes. "My arm—I can't—" he murmured in a stilted rasp followed by a pained sob. "Please don't make me move it."

CHAPTER 18

"It's good that we found them when we did," said Dr. Carver to the nurse at his side as they strolled between the rows of empty beds, stopping at the last two, and looking on either side at the sleeping patients with quiet satisfaction. A tranquil morning shone through the high windows, its silver radiance lending a hallowed touch to the room and its white linen.

Another nurse, who had finished checking one of the patient's vital signs, stepped back to let the doctor approach the head of the bed, where the patient lay with his eyes closed, looking more at peace than when he and his companion first staggered through the double doors of the derelict ward and into the hands of the orderlies stationed nearby. He had been bleeding from various cuts and injuries, and the younger inmate with him had his arm wrapped in a makeshift sling, made with the former's tattered coveralls.

The sedative they were given before receiving treatment still had its hold on them, and so Carver took this chance to poke a long swab between the sleeping patient's parted lips, taking care not to induce a gag reflex as he scraped his teeth and the inside of his cheek, before extracting the swab to peer over his glasses at red stains on the cotton wad.

As he turned and headed for the second patient's bed, Greg's eyelids twitched and drew back with a dull ache to bright and blurred surroundings.

"No, this confirms it," he heard, and weakly turned his head towards the source of the voice, who had his back turned as he bent over a patient in the opposite bed, examining something before presenting it to the nurse.

"Look at that. Traces of it here too. I doubt an analysis is necessary. I suppose that's why it didn't take with him. This one will have to go back."

He turned towards Greg, who instinctively lowered his lids, pretending to be asleep.

"This one, however, is to be tagged once he recovers. He might have taken a dose, it's true, but I've examined him already, and at this stage it won't make much of a difference apart from acting as an anticoagulant. It put him at risk, given his injuries, but the transfusion helped and he's past that now."

Carver's hand hovered over Greg's face with the intent of checking in the inside of his eyelids. But at the last moment he decided it was best not to push it and retracted his hand.

"It won't be long before he's at the same stage as Wyatt," said Carver, resuming his soliloquy as he and the nurse headed to the door. "Which reminds me, I'll have to find a replacement for him: he's well into the advanced stage…" his voice trailed off as the two of them disappeared into hallway.

Greg sat up, craning his neck to glance at the door before

turning to the bed facing him, where Nader slept with one arm in a sling, and the other cuffed to the bed rail. Like him, Greg had one arm cuffed to the bed rail while the other was hooked to an IV drip. But this was for the moment forgotten as Greg examined his bare arms, hideously mottled and bruised as they were, turning them over in speechless wonder after he had given up hope of ever seeing his own skin again.

He must have been out cold when they had removed that damned suit, though he couldn't imagine how it was done, let alone done without rousing him in the process.

It was still daytime when he opened his eyes again after sinking unawares into a dreamless sleep. He found a nurse removing the IV catheter from his arm and asked where they were.

The nurse smiled down kindly on him, gathered the empty IV bag, used catheter, and crumpled adhesive strips, and left without answering.

A minute later Carver came in rolling a table with a covered food tray. He sat on the edge of Greg's bed, bringing the table closer, and upon seeing Greg raise himself to a sitting position while eyeing the tray with interest, Carver pushed the table back and said: "First I want you to answer a few questions, if you don't mind."

Greg rolled his eyes as he sank back into bed and rolled onto his side.

"Never a free lunch with you, is it?" he grumbled from the depth of the covers he had pulled up.

"My questions are few, so the sooner you give me straight answers, the sooner you can eat. First of all, where did you get those capsules?"

"What capsules?" asked Greg, still with his back turned.

"These," said Carver, pulling a brown bottle out of his coat pocket and rolling out a few red capsules onto his palm. Greg looked over his shoulder at the capsules, then stole an involuntary glance at Nader, intuiting from the untouched tray near him that in all likelihood he had remained asleep and therefore had not been questioned yet. Whether or not Carver had caught him glancing at Nader was unknown to Greg, though a sidelong look showed the doctor occupied in that brief moment with returning the capsules back into the bottle.

"If you're going to take shots in the dark about who broke into your secret stash, you might want to start with your staff first," said Greg, turning away again.

Carver sat back and crossed his arms with a look of skepticism. "There were traces of it in your mouth," he said, and when Greg did not answer the doctor, turning to one side of the room, called: "Nurse? You may take his tray now."

After a moment, Greg sat up. "Look, if you're asking me who the dealer was, then I don't know. All I know is he carried me to the staff quarters while I was out cold, dumped me in the tub, and then left me a message on tape. I never saw his face."

"And where is that tape?"

Greg scratched the back of his head, trying to remember. "I think I left it back in that run-down section."

"Yes, you were lucky we found you when we did," said Carver, tapping forehead over his right eye, and Greg mechanically mirrored the gesture, touching the bandage that covered the stitches over his left eyebrow. His gaze then dropped to his covered feet, and Carver pulled back the blanket to show his bandaged foot.

"Yes, seems like you cut yourself on a large piece of glass..."

"It wasn't broken glass," said Greg, fixing him with a look.

"There were glass shards in the wound when we cleaned it," returned Carver. "Why? What else could have caused it?"

If the answer was on the tip of Greg's tongue, it was checked by Carver's expression as he leaned in, as if anticipating a crazy anecdote, which he would hear with wide-eyed attentiveness and a series of slow, understanding nods before summoning one of the nurses to ask her, in an aside, to fetch the orderlies and a straight-jacket.

"Alright, so it was broken glass. Can I have my meal now? Also, I don't think these are necessary." He held up his manacled hand, clanking the cuff against the bed rail.

"Safety measures," said Carver. "There was an unfortunate incident a while ago in which a nurse was assaulted by one of the inmates here in this ward. Ever since then we've taken precautions to avoid future incidents from recurring."

Greg leaned in and spoke with the air of divulging a plain fact that for some reason was difficult for his listener to absorb: "I'm not an inmate here, and I'm not going to attack anyone. And neither will he," he added, indicating Nader.

"Yes, a curious case that one," said Carver, looking over his shoulder at Nader. "His arm was gouged in several places with a sharp tool in a manner almost similar to one of the orderlies, the one whom you encountered in the apartments."

It took a few seconds for the hint to sink in.

"Wait a minute—I didn't—!" stammered Greg, looking alarmed. "I mean, sure, I'll take the blame for the orderly. But Nader—his arm was already mangled by the time I found him."

"Are you sure?" said Carver. "How do you know you weren't

having an episode when it happened?"

"An episode? An episode of what?"

Instead of explaining, Carver reached for his coat's inner pocket and pulled out the black tape recorder.

"The tape you had in here. I assume you've heard the whole thing."

"What does that—"

"Answer the question, please."

Greg paused a moment before answering: "Some parts here and there."

"Did it sound familiar?"

"I didn't make those recordings."

Carver smiled at this. "After all, they were made by your double. He was leaving messages to a former staff member by the name of Holden. If I was asking you about the capsules, it's because Holden administered them without my knowledge or approval to patients here under the misguided notion that he was helping them. Unfortunately, many of them suffered adverse effects. The drugs in these capsules have blood thinning properties—but they can also induce a psychotic episode. It happened with a few inmates, two of whom showed violent tendencies. I mentioned an incident in which a nurse was attacked by one of the inmates—well, he was given one of those capsules. So, how can you say with any certainty that you didn't attack your friend there?"

For a while, Greg stared down at his free hand, resting in his lap.

"Because I didn't have anything sharp on me when I found him. It was—"

"It was—?" repeated Carver, but Greg withdrew into baffled

silence.

If his foot injury was caused by broken glass and the whole encounter was nothing more than a psychotic episode, then who or what ran off with his knife?

"This whole situation is a mess, my friend, but perhaps you can help me turn it around. You see, we've already apprehended the perpetrator, but he won't admit to anything. Now I believe he's the one behind the shooting, but I have no evidence for this. We can neither find the gun nor any other incriminating evidence."

Greg fixed the doctor with a knowing look. A moment ago, he would have asked why the police weren't involved yet; but all at once, he knew it would never happen.

"Vigilantism, doctor? Is that how you do things around here?"

"All I want is information. This should interest you as well—it involves your double. I'm sure you've guessed by now he wasn't an ordinary inmate. Our perpetrator, Holden, was working with him. And being a staff member at the time meant that Holden could smuggle in or hold on to things for him—a weapon, for example. And also this—"

Here Carver reached for the black bundle, unrolled it, and held up the Skins for Greg to see, though he might as well have held up an explosive device the way Greg flinched back at the sight of it.

"How did—" he began, staring at the undone zipper, running diagonally from shoulder to hip, its metal teeth misaligned in a warped grin. The suit had reverted to its original shape, without any trace of the small adamantine plates that once projected through the fabric and covered him like scales; now it looked almost like an ordinary wetsuit, albeit one made with fine, scaly material.

"I believe this belonged to your double," Carver continued, seemingly deaf to the stammered question. "It's your size, after all. Right now, we have Holden sedated in another room. We tried questioning him, and in the process, he bit his tongue. I believe he was trying to chew it off." He paused to enjoy the sight of muted horror on Greg's face. "But, if we catch him at the right moment, when he's just waking up, groggy and confused, I have a feeling the sight of you in that suit will loosen that tongue of his. I'm sure he has a few choice words to say—"

"I'm not putting it on," Greg broke out.

The remark surprised Carver. "But you were wearing it when they brought you in," he said, bringing the suit close to test the young man's reaction.

"It almost killed me," murmured Greg, aware of how ridiculous he sounded; still, he tensed up when the suit was laid across his knees, as though it were a venomous snake.

"This?" asked Carver, sticking his arm through the sleeve to prove its harmlessness. Greg appeared ready to bolt at the slightest trigger, but there was a subtle shift in his expression.

"You forget, my friend, that you were under the influence. Even now you'll find it hard to shake off what you believed then. It takes hold of you like a vivid nightmare. You'll just have to prove to yourself it wasn't real."

Greg flashed him an uneasy smile. "Easier said than done."

"This is all necessary to track down your double. We only get one chance at this, so it has to be right. Holden's obstinate: the harder we questioned him, the more tight-lipped he grew.

If we want information, we'll have to coax it out of him."

"And what do I get from all this?"

Carver seemed taken aback by the question. "Don't you want to apprehend him? Your double, I mean. After all, he likely ran off with your personal items—your wallet, your phone… I'm sure you're eager to get them back."

"I'd rather take my chances reporting identity theft and having everything reissued," Greg rejoined.

Carver swept his hand to dismiss the idea. "Oh, that will take time—money. I doubt you could afford it. Somehow I get the impression you're unemployed. You never once mentioned having a job to get back to…"

"That's none of your business."

"What I meant was if there's nothing urgent to call you back out there, why not stay with us? I can arrange for more comfortable accommodations—you can stay in this ward: the food is better." He uncovered the food tray to reveal a plate heaped with pancakes and eggs, sausages, tomatoes, and a ramekin of fruit cocktail. "The orderlies and inmates won't bother you here, and the nurses will look after you."

Greg tried to articulate a smart comeback, but the sight of this breakfast cornucopia held his tongue. The smell alone was enough to turn his head, and the idea of being well-fed, well-rested, and well-cared for was too good for him not to stop and consider, especially when nothing but trouble awaited him outside. Carver was right: what was his hurry when it would be more convenient to wait for the thief to be brought here with all his belongings instead of having to report the theft and have everything replaced or reissued?

But he caught himself piling on one excuse after another,

building a case for accepting Carver's offer—an offer nonetheless too easy, too convenient not to be suspect.

"Think it over," said Carver, pushing the tray closer as he rose to leave. "I need to go make my rounds now, but I'll come back later for your answer."

Not long after Carver had left, two nurses came in to switch Greg to leg cuffs that chained him to the sturdy base of the bed, but granted him the liberty of walking around. If it was a gesture of good will, it was a welcome one, as Greg was unable to sit still while thinking. Presently he hobbled back and forth in front of his bed, arms crossed and hands tucked under them for warmth, while the long chain clinked around his bare ankles.

Somehow the excellent breakfast he had enjoyed, and the nurses, who smiled and flirted in their own manner as they replaced one set of chains for another, all worked inadvertently to make Carver's offer seem more dubious than appealing. Like a generous promise, the more attractive it was, the more suspect it became; Greg was almost certain he would see none of it as soon as he played his part and handed Carver what he wanted; once his usefulness was spent, what's to keep the good doctor from throwing him back in his cell?

Greg chafed the back of his head in frustration. What if he was being paranoid? After all, Carver could have easily promised to release him without any intention of fulfilling it. But this was Carver—Janus-faced, manipulative Carver who detained him on false pretenses. If he refused to involve outside authorities, it was because of some illicit operation being carried out here. And apparently in the doctor's eyes, Greg knew or had seen too much—maybe not enough for him to get a full picture, but enough to make Carver unwilling to release him. It was never about maintaining order, as Carver had claimed. But much like that first evening, Greg found himself with no bargaining chips to discuss his terms. And here he was, chained to a bed, being asked to interrogate another inmate for valuable information—

He stopped, lifting his lowered head with sudden realization. Valuable information: that was his bargaining chip.

Carver couldn't be in the same room with him while he spoke to Holden—not if he wanted to keep up the act. Which meant whatever he gleaned from his talk with Holden he could use to bargain for his freedom. Only he would have to be smart about it if he didn't want to end up like Holden.

CHAPTER 19

Carver paced the corridor, waiting for Greg, who joined him a minute later, dressed in the black suit.

The doctor surveyed him with a nod of approval—even barefoot, the young man looked imposing and bellicose in this strange outfit—and began going over the plan, reiterating the finer details.

While he spoke, Greg kept his absent gaze fixed at a spot where the floor met the wall. Prior to getting dressed, he had gone to use the bathroom and was alarmed to find his urine clouded with red. Whether it was discolored or mixed with blood it was hard to say, though as he washed his hands, Greg tried to convince himself that it was probably the former, and the discoloration was due to the capsule's red dye. Even if it were blood, the drug had blood-thinning properties, and anticoagulants were known to cause blood in the urine. It was probably nothing.

Still, he surfaced from his ruminations on the verge of asking

Carver about it; but instead, the doctor was looking at him as if anticipating an answer to something.

"What?" asked Greg, having missed the question and everything else that preceded it.

Carver gave an exasperated sigh. "I'll give you the abridged version. Over there—" pointing to a door farther down the corridor—"is Holden's room. He should be up by now. When you talk to him, I want you to go along with whatever he says. The idea is to keep him talking. Just don't get sucked into his madness. Bear in mind you're talking to someone mired in their delusions. You might be lucid now, there's a small chance traces of the drug are still in your system, enough to cloud your judgement. I would have preferred to wait longer if we weren't short on time. I'll be monitoring the situation in case—"

"Monitoring?" interrupted Greg. "Why monitoring?"

Carver compressed his mouth by way of a shrug. "It's just a safety measure. You might need to loosen his restraints to convince him you're his ally. But things could get out of hand—Holden could try to escape, or he might be holding a grudge against your double and decide to act on it. But don't worry: if something goes wrong, you can be sure the orderlies will be barging in to intervene. Now then, off you go."

He turned and left, leaving Greg to stare after him with the sickening sense of having lost his foothold before he had the chance to have a secure hold on the ledge.

Then again, he thought, relaxing a fraction, *then again, monitoring might not mean listening in, and whatever info I get remains exclusive to me.*

You hold on to that happy thought, said a voice in him.

The room was dark when Greg opened the door, and light

spilling in from the hallway revealed a wall facing the door, which served to partition the entryway from the rest of the room, giving a sense of privacy reserved for VIP suites.

He spotted the black dome of a security camera mounted in one corner of the room, guessed another was mounted in the opposite corner, and wondered whether or not Holden would likewise note their presence and refuse to talk.

As he shut the door, Greg heard someone call from behind the partition wall.

"That better not be a tray of swill you're bringing in," slurred the voice, giving Greg pause before he spoke.

"It's me," he said, and remembering the tapes added, "kemosabe," almost in an afterthought.

"Grim?" answered Holden after a moment's hesitation.

Greg stopped to consider the word before deciding from the inflection that it was his double's name—if not a nickname bestowed by Holden—and it occurred to him then that he never got his double's name from Carver; but now that Holden voluntarily supplied it, there was no point in dwelling over it.

"Who else?" said Greg, emerging from behind the partition to resume his role. His eyes were still adjusting to the dark, but he could almost discern the bed where Holden lay. To Greg, there was something reassuring about the relative cover of dark: he could try to assume Grim's way of talking as best as he could, but the small tics, gestures, and expressions could give him away if he was not careful.

"Well, you seem surprised I came back for you," Greg added when it seemed Holden wasn't going to speak.

"There's a light switch on the wall to your right," said Holden. "Turn it on."

"Why? We're more secure in the dark."

"Just do it," Holden insisted. "I want to see who I'm talking to."

Reluctantly, Greg went back to the door, flipped the light switch, then returned and stopped short when he saw Holden and realized he had seen him before. Under the glare of lights, Holden squinted at Greg through bruised eyelids, while Greg stared back at the inmate from the food fight in the dining hall, who now lay back, strapped to his bed by a five-point restraint.

"What brings you back?" said Holden. "I thought you'd be on your way out by now."

Greg broke his gaze and took a few steps, stalling while he gathered his scattered thoughts. After all, if he and Holden had met before, albeit on such hostile terms, where did that put them? Was there even a point in continuing the charade?

"You said you wanted me to find you," answered Greg, now remembering a portion of the message Holden had left him.

Holden blinked, trying to remember. "I did?"

"You said you'd return the gun once I got better," said Greg, gaining confidence from Holden's uncertainty.

"I'm a little groggy right now," said Holden. "Help me with these." He indicated the leather restraints with his head, and Greg checked an impulse to glance back at the surveillance cameras before approaching the bed.

"So, where's the gun?" Greg asked, taking his time with the strap.

"Had to get rid of it. Didn't want Carver to find it…"

"Get rid of it how? Did you toss it in a garbage chute? Or—"

"Would you hurry up with that?"

"I'm trying!" Greg snapped back. "They've got them on

tight."

"Yeah, no shit. I think they're hoping to cut off circulation."

"If you can complain, you can think."

"I can't think when I'm flat on my back."

"There," said Greg, sliding the leather strap through the buckle.

"About time," beamed Holden, opening and closing his hand, and shaking his arm. "Now the other. To be honest, I didn't think you'd make a detour to help me out. I'd have expected you'd take the capsules and run."

"Couldn't leave without my gun," rejoined Greg, and Holden snorted as if to say "of course not."

Once both cuffs were loosened, Holden took care of the larger middle strap around his waist.

"Well, I'm sure your head's cleared up by now," said Greg, as Holden sat up in bed. He was starting to feel uneasy about the situation and had to remind himself that he was going along with Carver's suggestion to gain the man's trust.

"Give me a minute," said Holden, shrugging one shoulder after the other and tilting his head. Then his eyes fell on Greg and he looked at him as if seeing him for the first time. "What happened to your uniform?"

The question caught Greg off guard, and he glanced down at the black suit, thinking Holden was referring to the Skins before realizing he meant the grey coveralls.

"Does it matter now? We're short on time here…"

"Short on time?" Holden scoffed, as if he couldn't believe the audacity of the remark. "When you nagged on and on about being careful not to blow your cover?"

"Yeah, well, you blew my cover the moment you went

trigger-happy and started shooting people left and right."

"Trigger-hap—!" echoed the other before the words got choked by an incredulous laugh. "Don't you tell me about blowing your precious cover when I did that to save your sorry ass. If I hadn't done that, you'd be a few doors down from here by now, drooling in a cup. I kept my mouth shut—Carver couldn't get anything out of me. Even if he suspected something, he wouldn't have tied the gun or anything back to you—at least not until you sauntered in with that damned rig of yours just to tell me how I blew your precious cover."

"Look," said Greg, trying to diffuse the situation before it spiraled out of control, "all I'm saying is there's no point in hiding now that Carver suspects something's up."

But the effect was like dousing grease fire with water. For a moment Holden could only stare back with an apoplectic half-grin; then he spoke with a dreadful calm.

"Wait, let me see if I got this right: after all that tap dancing we did—after all the hoops you made me jump through—you're saying you no longer care if Carver knows what's coming."

"Come on," smiled Greg, trying on a grifter's charm, "you think I'm careless enough to throw caution to the wind? I took a risk, but it was a calculated risk. Carver will still get what's coming to him." He hadn't the slightest clue what Holden was referring to, but still recognized the need for reassurance, keeping his response vague enough for Holden to read into it whatever he wanted to hear. The words had their desired effect, and while Holden still fixed him with a look of anger, it was anger cowed into silence.

"Now about that gun…" Greg tried again.

Holden mumbled something.

"Come again?" said Greg, noticing a glint in Holden's eyes he didn't like.

"I said what type of gun are we talking here?"

"A handgun, of course."

"You'll have to be more specific."

"I don't have time for twenty questions."

"It'll only take a second if you can tell me what model it was. I'll make it easier: was it a revolver or a semi-automatic?"

"Semi-automatic," answered Greg, on the notion that a revolver seemed incongruous with the suit he wore.

"Very good. What calibre?"

Greg thought back to the bodies in the hallway, trying to estimate the size of the bullet from the wounds.

".45 calibre," he ventured.

A hoarse chuckle rattled in the inmate's chest. "Oh, you almost had me, I'll give you that. So how about you stop pretending and tell me who you really are."

The remark landed on Greg like a hail of needles, yet his expression remained unflinching.

"I'm not playing your games, kemosabe."

"Don't kemosabe me. Where's Grim?"

In spite of himself, one corner of Greg's mouth twitched into a half-smile: once called out, he could not for the life of him maintain a bluff. "Grim's no longer with us."

"Gone or dead?"

"I wouldn't expect a postcard from him if I were you."

"And you are?"

Greg shrugged. "Just a bonehead filling his shoes—so to speak."

"Except you work for Carver now."

"I'm not working for Carver."

"Whatever. We're done talking here. So, why don't you run back to Carver and tell him where next to stick his hand now that he's done playing you for a puppet."

"Tell him yourself: he's been listening in this whole time," said Greg, tilting his head to indicate one of the security cameras, which Holden regarded with a snort of contempt.

"Not unless he can lip read—which I doubt he could from that distance. He's watching, sure, but he can't hear us. It's why I asked you to turn on those lights. Sounds crazy, doesn't it? There's a reason Grim chose to work with me. I might be a custodian, but I could do more than just mop floors, you know. Who do you think knows the ins and outs of this place? The building's more porous than you might think. My specialty was finding those crawlspaces and passages, and pointing them out to Carver. Without me he'd have had more than one missing inmate to worry about. Not that I told him everything, of course, but it was enough to earn his trust. And I was largely ignored unless I was called to clean up or repair things, which meant I could rewire a few things without drawing attention. That switch, for example—it cuts off the audio whenever the lights are on. And I bet you the old dog's over in the surveillance room, fiddling with dials and pressing buttons trying to figure why he's not getting any sound."

Greg followed Holden's gaze, looking towards the camera. "So, whatever went on here was just between the two of us?"

"Us and these walls," Holden assented.

Greg couldn't help a small laugh of relief, clapping his hands together. "You're beautiful, Holden, you know that? You just did me a solid without knowing it."

Holden shrugged off the tribute. "I doubt it when it's your ass they'll be hauling away for a thorough debriefing. I imagine the rickety bastard will want to hear everything since he didn't get to listen in. Except you won't have much to say, and he'll suspect you of holding back—that's when he'll call in the boys to apply themselves to whatever method would get you to talk."

"Whatever, Holden, I'm out," said Greg, inwardly considering bolting for the door before the orderlies arrived—and then remembering at the last moment that he wouldn't get far with his injured foot. And he didn't get far either starting for the door, when Holden, in one swift motion, sprang out of bed and ambushed Greg, grabbing him by the throat and pinning him to the wall.

But Greg was prompt to slam the heel of his hand into Holden's face, followed by a head bash that sent the other staggering back. Greg then threw himself at Holden's back, locking him in a choke hold.

The larger man stooped and doubled over, trying to throw him off, but Greg had his legs clasped around Holden's waist and held on, even as Holden slammed his back against the wall. Finally he elbowed Greg's side, hitting a sore spot. With a sharp cry, Greg lost his grip, and was promptly thrown off.

He struggled to his feet, only to receive a succession of punches that left him tottering a few moments, glaring at Holden while trying to remain on his feet. But the ground swayed underfoot, and the clumsy punch he threw back was easily sidestepped by Holden, who decked Greg once more and felled him.

When Greg opened his eyes, and his vision began to clear, he found Holden leaning his full weight against the door. The pounding from the other side spoke of the orderlies' arrival and attempt at breaking in. And while the door was locked, evinced by the door knob, which rattled but never turned, Holden still seemed to find it necessary to bodily barricade the door.

"Hey!" Holden called when he noticed Greg opening his eyes, "if you know what's good for you, you'll bring that bed here."

Greg dropped his throbbing head back and ignored him.

"Look—not that I care for your welfare," Holden went on, "but once they get their hands on you, it won't take much to crack you open, and what little you know might still compromise things."

"I'd say the situation is beyond compromise now," said Greg with a groan as he staggered to his feet, holding his side.

"You'd think I'd back myself into a corner with no exits?" said Holden, and after considering: "Well, maybe I would, but I have something up my sleeve now if you'll work with me."

Greg, however, pretended not to hear, and kept his frowning attention on the back of his hand, which came back smeared red after wiping it against his bleeding nose.

Meanwhile, the pounding grew louder, more concentrated around the door knob. It was enough to unnerve Greg—he knew Holden was right: they were coming for him.

He kept staring at the door with growing unease, which must have manifested on his face, since Holden repeated: "Listen, we can help each other." And when Greg still looked doubtful, he added: "Did Carver promise treatment? A cure for your condition? Is that why you're doing this? 'Cause I gotta tell you the cure he has in mind is not the cure you're hoping for."

The door began to show signs of being stoved, or so it seemed to Greg, who went to the other side of the room and began to drag the iron rail bed. It took some effort to drive it into the slip of a hall, but after Holden left his post to clear the way—hoping the lock would hold in the meantime—together they wedged the bed between the door and the partition wall.

"What condition?" asked Greg after a silent pause in which they stood eyeing the barricade.

Holden gave him a quizzical look. "You don't know? You don't feel anything?"

"You mean from the drug?"

"What drug?"

"Those red capsules," said Greg. "Carver said you were giving them to inmates—said it was some kind of blood thinner. I mean, look at this—it's like a leaky faucet." He touched his bloodied nose to illustrate. "I took one yesterday and felt a surge of energy at first, and then I began to hallucinate."

Holden tipped his head to one side, considering Greg. Something in that look did not bode well: had Holden been quick to dismiss Carver's claims, it might have asserted the doctor's verdict that Holden was delusional; instead the inmate seemed to evaluate the case before him with a touch of hesitation, and there was something lucid about the way he deliberated before answering.

"You weren't experiencing those symptoms from the drug itself," he said. "You've had them because it's reacting to whatever's incubating inside you."

To Greg, the words evoked a memory of the thing he had vomited in the sink—a memory that by now had the quality of a vivid nightmare. He heard himself chuckle, or at least give a hollow, humorless rasp. "Bullshit. I didn't have those symptoms until I took the drug."

His reaction elicited a look of concern from Holden, who almost sounded apologetic as he answered: "If you were clean, you wouldn't have had that reaction from it."

A few moments of silence passed, through which Holden noted the absence of the pounding and realized the orderlies must have left to fetch an axe or something to break down the door.

"Look, I wish I could tell you everything I know, but we need to move now," said Holden. "Turn off the lights and follow me. And keep your voice down."

After the lights were off, Holden led Greg to a spot where the bed once stood, then motioned him to crouch down and pry away the loosened wooden floorboards. Greg followed suit, working mechanically while his mind remained preoccupied.

"This condition—" Greg faltered in a low voice, "how serious is it?"

"It's degenerative," said Holden. "If there's a treatment, you won't find it here. Carver likes them docile and quiet."

"Docile and quiet how?"

"You'll see. Alright, that's all of them," he said, putting away the last floorboard. "Get in."

"Get in where?"

"The crawlspace," said Holden, giving Greg a push towards the narrow hole that now yawned before him.

"You ever been down one these crawlspaces?" hissed Greg. "They're crawling with things—and I don't mean rats or roaches…"

"You have any other options, princess?"

"There's two of us. We could fight our way out."

"Yeah—well—unless you're immune to the effects of mace and stun guns, I suggest you move," answered Holden, grabbing the back of Greg's head to shove him down.

"If you're so confident," gritted Greg between his set teeth, resisting Holden's push, "why not go in first?"

"Trust me, if I could, I would have nosedived in there and crawled out ages ago."

"Everything you've said—how do I know it's true? I'm not even sure I trust you."

The pressure on his head eased as Holden relented. "You trust Carver?"

"I don't, but—at least he didn't leave a trail of dead bodies in his wake."

"None that you've seen yet," qualified Holden sardonically. "Besides, my letting you go should be enough reason to trust me. If you want proof, you'll find it out there—the stuff you'll find in Carver's office alone has it in spades. You'll need to head there anyway to get those capsules."

"What for?"

"Wish I could say they're a cure, but at this point, all they can do is buy you time until you can get some proper medical attention. You said your last dose was yesterday, so you'll need to take one as soon as possible, before narcolepsy sets in. Now listen: this crawlspace connects to a maintenance tunnel, which will lead you to a utility room. Don't worry if the end of the tunnel looks blocked; one of the old janitors had a cupboard there to cover the hole in the wall. You'll be able to push it out of the way. When you get out, find a staircase, go one floor down, and head to Carver's office. He keeps confiscated items there, and I'm sure the capsules are no exception. Take one as soon as you get your hands on it. At this point I can't say what effect it might have on you: might help—might make you sick—hell, might even kill you if you OD on them—not that you have any reason to. But it's your best bet. Now move before I bury you down that hole."

Holden waited for Greg to disappear down the crawlspace, and then began replacing the floorboards.

CHAPTER 20

It was cold enough for the boy to see his breath: clouds floated before the pale orange light that seeped in under the door. He blew out breath after breath as he lay under his wool blanket and watched as those misty billows caught the scant light. For a while, the world seemed void of anything but him and those dying wisps of breath.

It was as Holden had said: the end of the narrow passageway was blocked by a cupboard, which Greg began shoving out of the way, stopping to listen when something fell off the shelf, in case the noise drew someone's attention. He then went on pushing until he had enough space to squeeze out.

The small utility room stored brooms, mops, and cleaning products, and had little to offer apart from an emergency flashlight and a screwdriver, both of which Greg pocketed.

After surveying the bright corridor, trying to decide which way would lead him to the stairs, Greg tried the left path. Not far, however, he began to hear the powerful thwacks of an axe cleaving through the door to Holden's room, and doubled back to go the other way.

He narrowed his eyes against the fluorescent lights, scanning the white walls for signs that could point him to the stairway, when he passed by a large communal room, lined with eight beds, four to each row, arranged so that both rows faced each other. And in a likewise symmetrical manner, inmates reclined in each bed, resting their plump hands in their laps while they stared into space with a wistful smile, as though savoring some distant and perhaps unearthly delight.

Greg had no intention of lingering, and yet his feet seemed to carry him of their own accord as he stepped between the beds, looking right and left at each round face and upturned, half-closed eyes before noting their reflective orange armbands, the sole streak of vital color against the grey sleeves and amidst the whites and pale greens of the room.

Somewhere deep within the room, one of them hummed quietly to himself, a solitary sound droning through the profound silence. It came from the last bed to the right, where an inmate (almost marring the symmetry of the room) lay covered with a blanket, his head obscured from view by the dividing curtains.

The faint humming brought to mind Clark, whom Greg half-expected to see as he approached the last bed, and was baffled when instead he found Hitch lying there, his eyes rolled back and semi-closed, showing curves of white like two thin crescents under each lowered lid, his lips parted with the onset of the same smile shared by his roommates.

The sight absorbed Greg until, like a touch on his shoulder, he sensed someone's presence, and turned to find a nurse standing between the rows of beds, staring at him with a look of mild surprise.

"Could you help me, miss?" he heard himself say before she had time to react. "I'm looking for Dr. Carver and thought I'd find him here. He's been expecting me to report back to him regarding the inmate in room 302."

As he spoke, he maintained eye contact to project an air of honesty. Where this came from he couldn't say; yet he spoke like he was following a rehearsed script, and even managed a subtle smile, as if the sight of her was a welcome one. Inwardly, however, he was holding himself back from springing to catch her: if she suspected something—if she were to turn around and run to alert someone—he had little to no chance of stopping her, not while a hurried hobble was all he could manage. But as long as he kept talking, as long as he kept her engaged while he drew ever closer to have her within lunging distance…

"I was told to meet him in his office below if I can't find him here," he went on, hoping his knowledge of the office location would make him seem more trustworthy. Though he was not in grey like the inmates, he had a sense being clad in black did not make him seem less hostile; and trying to seem disarming, he indicated his bandaged foot and added with a self-deprecating smile: "If it's no trouble, I was hoping you could escort me to it? I lost my crutch, you see, and I'd welcome the assistance."

At that point, he was close enough to get a whiff of the subtle scent she wore, and while she glanced down at his foot, he almost lunged at her, but hesitated at the crucial moment and lost his chance as she lifted her eyes to him.

Her gaze was spacey yet canny, as if everything around her

filtered through a wall of apathy; at any rate, it showed no signs of alarm or that she suspected anything. Perhaps she knew he was collaborating with Carver, but was not yet aware of his recent defection. And just when he was starting to feel uneasy under her prolonged scrutiny, she twined her arm in his, and gently led him out.

As they went down the corridor, he stared ahead, unseeing, his senses bristling and focused on the blind spots, tuned to any sound or disturbance coming from there. The diminishing strikes of the axe behind them reassured him somewhat, but what if someone crossed their path? What then?

He remembered the screwdriver was within reach if he needed to use it, but it was not much of a deterrent, unless pointed at a hostage… At the thought, he cast an uneasy side glance at the nurse, then pushed the idea away, hoping it would not come to that.

Her hand, which nestled in the hollow of his elbow, now curled over his bicep in a familiar way. It was a subtle shift, but it caught him off guard. Suddenly he was aware of her hand, and the vital warmth radiating from it, and all his perceptions, which he had thrown outward, now seemed involuntarily drawn to it.

Distracted at that instant, he failed to notice the nurses' station they were approaching, until a matronly nurse, who sat behind the desk, stood up as they passed her by.

Greg caught her gaze for a brief moment before looking away, as if avoiding eye contact somehow made him less visible. The nurse at his side, however, smiled at the older nurse and walked on, as though the man at her side was a patient being taken for a rehabilitating stroll.

It took but a few seconds to pass her by, yet somehow

Greg knew that was not the end of it. And sure enough, in a backwards glance, he saw the older nurse emerging from the station, calling out to them to stop.

The nurse at his side stifled a giggle, and he felt her arm tighten around his as she broke into a sprint and pulled him along. He struggled to keep up, stumbling more than running, surprised at the strength of the smaller nurse as she held him up and kept him from falling.

They rounded a corner and ducked into the day room, drawing the brief and languid attention of a handful of inmates who lounged there, each in his choice spot.

Greg, still catching his breath, turned to the nurse and was about to say something when she cupped her hands over his mouth to silence him, and glanced out into the hallway, stifling another laugh, as if the two of them had just shared an absurd joke.

He drew her hands away. "Miss, I don't have time for—" he began in an undertone, trailing off when he noticed the ID badge pinned to her cardigan showed a photo of a different nurse. But before he had time to form any conclusions, the older nurse's anxious calls came from the hallway outside. Seconds later, she stood panting in the doorway, surveying the day room for a moment before stepping in search of the runaway pair.

Greg watched her surreptitiously from behind a wide sofa, which seated a row of heavy inmates. She turned his way and he ducked back to hide from view, at which point he realized the young nurse (or whoever she was) was no longer at his side.

The older nurse, seeming to have noticed him, called out for them to come out. When neither of them answered, she approached his hiding spot. Greg waited for her to come close enough and then crept around to the opposite side, hoping to sneak past her while she checked behind the sofa.

But as she walked past the seated inmates, one of them reached down and caught the hem of her long skirt.

"Tell me I'm handsome," he pleaded, looking up at her.

She swatted his hand, but he held on and insisted. Irritated, she snatched her skirt free, and then jumped with a shrill cry when the younger nurse stole behind her and playfully clapped her hands on the older nurse's shoulders.

After recovering, the older nurse began to reprimand her subordinate, who kept her eyes cast down in feigned remorse, twisting her mouth to one side to suppress a guilty smile. She then relinquished the borrowed nursing cap and cardigan; like the inmates, she wore coveralls, though hers was of a lighter shade

Again, the seated inmate reached for the older nurse's skirt, demanding attention. Again she fended him off as she ushered the female patient out. The patient followed behind, but fell back a step as she reached the doorway, where, in one fluid motion, she swiveled on her heels to look in Greg's general direction, waggling her fingers to wave goodbye.

Greg, who watched this from his hiding place, reciprocated with an uncertain wave; but by then she had turned away and left. He waited a moment, and when it seemed no one was coming here to look for him, he cautiously stepped out of his hiding place and headed to the doorway.

The same inmate, leaning forward, caught his hand and pleaded: "Tell me I'm handsome."

Greg freed his hand, but stooped to level his eyes with the

inmate, and said: "You're the handsomest that ever was. And don't let anyone tell you otherwise."

With that, he limped out of the day room and went to find the stairway.

Nader, his good hand and ankles strapped to a wheelchair, was being taken back to his cell by one of the nurses, when with a choked cry, the wheelchair came to a sudden stop.

He turned to look back and felt a contending mixture of relief and alarm when he found Clark standing behind the nurse, pressing a knife to her throat, his upper lip and right cheek smeared with blood.

CHAPTER 21

Having descended the stairs one floor down, Greg peered down at the angular spiral of the stairs below, clasping the banister as though keeping himself anchored against the urge to continue his descent, find the nearest exit, and run. Nothing guaranteed those stairs would lead him to the lobby with its double doors—or even a back door—the place might not even be as deserted as it had been before. Still, what was to keep him from trying his luck apart from Holden's injunction to make his way to Carver's office?

If it was about evidence, he'd already seen and experienced enough to know something was deeply wrong with the place; the irony was that it engendered more questions than answers. But then there was the matter of finding those capsules, along with Holden's claim they would buy him time. Though why buy time when he could escape if he managed to? It seemed a more direct route, until he considered the time it would take him to make his way down the mountain path on foot or even reach a hospital before narcolepsy set in partway and he collapsed in the middle of nowhere.

On the other hand, what if the capsules weren't as effective as Holden said they were, and the diversion proved to be a waste of time?

The indecisiveness left him wavering on the edge of the stairs. He patted the suit's pockets and dug through them, not sure what he was searching for until, with a deepening frown, he realized the handheld recorder was no longer with him. Not that he relied on it to make a decision, but it helped clear his mind when he thought out loud, and talking into a device did not carry the same stigma as talking to oneself—even if no one was around.

At length he heaved a sigh and pushed himself away from the banister, deciding that, after all, stabilizing his condition was first and foremost; besides, there was sure to be something of use in Carver's office, be it cash, or a set of master keys, or even a pair of shoes to help him cross the glass-littered grounds outside.

The lighting on this floor was softer and kinder to the eyes, and the doors here were recessed deep within the wall, granting him space to duck out of sight whenever a nurse or two passed by. So far, nurses were all he saw here, and given the homey aspect of the soft lights and papered walls, he guessed that this section housed their living quarters—which meant that Carver's office was in a different section. It had to be: the floors here were carpeted, and he didn't recall feeling anything of the like underfoot when Carver had led him to his office.

He hurried past an open door, catching a glimpse of a sunlit lounge area, where nurses sat reading in sofas or at tables or rested their elbows on the kitchenette counter, talking over steaming cups of coffee or tea.

The brief impression of this peaceful setting stayed with him, along with the scent of coffee, even as he crossed over to a different wing, found the door to Carver's office, and opened his eyes to find two or three nurses hovering over him while he lay with his head resting against the wall and his legs stretched out on the carpeted floor.

A tired-looking nurse holding a cup of coffee stood regarding him with detached curiosity while the other two, crouching on either side of him, pushed him down gently when he tried to get up. Their speech sounded garbled to his ears, but he understood from their tone and gesture that they were asking him to lie back down. For a confused moment he complied, not sure how he ended up here, thinking he must have fallen and hurt his head. Then he caught sight of one of the nurses darting an anxious glance towards one end of the hallway, and realized someone must have gone to fetch the orderlies for him.

Again, they tried to hold him down, but he pushed them out of the way in time to catch sight of the tired looking nurse lowering her cup with the intention of dousing him with hot coffee. He ducked to one side, avoiding the worst of it, which struck one of the nurses leaning over to subdue him. And while the other two turned their attention to their injured coworker, who shrank back, covering her scalded face, Greg staggered to his feet and half-stumbled, half-sprinted down the lopsided corridor.

He found refuge in the small linen room, where he hid behind the door, silently panting and squinting through the door crack for any pursuers.

When he was satisfied that no one had followed him, he turned his attention to his injured foot, which bled through the bandages, though it hardly grieved him while he ran. Or rather, the pain that hindered him before was now reduced to pinpricks whenever he applied some pressure on it. He undid the stained bandage, winced at the sight of the gaping wound, still tender and weeping. His foot felt feverish to the touch, and he placed his cold hands on it for a few moments, drawing some warmth from it before reaching for a clean cotton sheet from a nearby shelf, which he tore into bandage strips.

As he left, he discarded the old bandages down an intersecting hallway to throw off his scent and give the impression he went that way.

Eventually he reached an area where the carpeted floor stopped, marking a different section. There, he passed by a windowed door, and peered through the textured glass, which did not allow him a clear view of the room's interior, though it gave hints of red walls. The door was locked, but luckily the glass was not shatterproof, and having broken the window, Greg was able to reach his arm through and unlock it.

It was indeed Carver's office, but with an altered appearance: absent the stove fire animating the shadows, the office took on the stillness of a tomb, lit by a grid of square light fixtures that gave off a soft white light, and which Greg first mistook them for skylight windows, standing under them a moment with an upturned face, hoping to catch a glimpse of open sky.

He began his search with the large sturdy desk but found its shallow drawers contained little more than stationery. Next, he tried the bookcase for hidden compartments, at first pulling back one leather-bound volume at a time, then sweeping down rows of them all at once; a delicate touch seemed pointless considering the broken window.

At length he stood before the gutted bookcase with nothing

to show for his effort, and turning to step over the strewn books, caught a movement at the edge of his vision and froze. But it was nothing more than his image reflected in a full-length mirror, which hung in one corner of the room, almost hidden from view. He approached it and slid his hand along the recess between the wall and the mirror's black frame. There he found a raised switch, pressed it, and felt something release with a click before the mirror swung outward like a door.

He stepped through to a room overcrowded with boxes and furniture. Whatever scant sunlight came through the slit windows somehow made the room darker. At first it appeared to be a storeroom, and farther in he found a roll top desk and chair next to a squat sofa and a small side table. He ducked under a low wooden beam, traveling deeper towards the back, where he found an adjacent room with a single cot and its own bathroom.

Greg glanced over his shoulder to make sure the mirror door was still open before entering the adjacent room. Empty cans and bottles were piled in corners of the room. In one spot, ants had covered a half-eaten pastry and were dismantling it, ignoring the rotting fruit which had rolled under the cot, sprouting tufts of white and green mold. But for all that, a blanket was laid neatly folded on top of the cot, as if the owner was careful to make his bed before leaving.

His bed, Greg concluded, eyeing the two tailored suits, which hung from coat hangers on the wall behind him.

He went back to check the mirror door was still open, then returned to the bedroom.

"The capsules," he murmured, remembering why he came here. Under the bathroom's single light bulb, he rummaged through the medicine cabinet and found a plain brown bottle that stood out amongst the branded containers and labeled prescription bottles. As he uncapped the brown bottle to examine its contents, the lightbulb winked out, then returned with a dying glow, and he had to step out, seeking the scant sunlight, to get a better look at the contents of the bottle.

He checked the mirror door was still open, then raised the brown bottle to a thin ray of light and rattled it to release the red capsules stuck to the bottom of the glass.

Only about half a dozen of them were left.

He shook one out and swallowed it dry, pocketing the bottle with considerable relief.

Emerging from the bedroom, Greg paused before the closed roll top desk, tucked between stacks of boxes in this hidden, attic-like room. The mirror door was still ajar, with no sounds coming through it, and with that much assurance, Greg thought he might as well try this desk since it was hidden and, unlike its office counterpart, promised to hold more than stationery.

Indeed, when he pushed back the corrugated cover, he found a laptop sitting there with its screen folded over the keyboard, but not all the way, so that the operating system was still running.

"Finally, a lifeline." Greg smiled to himself, pushing back the screen as he sat down. A lifeline to what exactly, he couldn't say—it was more the idea of having a connection to the outside world. But his smile faded as soon as he saw the device was not connected to the internet, and recalled there was no service or working phone lines in the area.

"Dammit!" he hissed with an angry swipe at the desk. His sullen gaze fixed absently on an open browser window, until he realized he was looking at an email draft.

"As for the subjects," it began, "you leave men like that blowing in the wind and what happens? Like the social animals that they are, they tend to form a pack, and feel the need to be a part of something bigger. That's why they start to join gangs or groups. What draws these social outcasts and misfits? What glues them together? Acceptance. They want to be validated, vindicated for their views. If someone looks at them like they have potential, they're holding them by the heart—or other soft organs, if you prefer. They revert to being sons and brothers to their mentors. Their leader, the one with vision and dominant voice, preaches their anger and malcontent like it's the holy word. All at once, they feel like they belong to something bigger. You have enough people believing the same deluded thing and what happens? Extremists are born. Violence erupts. All because they found someone who validates their distorted views, if not exacerbates them.

"I am here to offer them a chance to be a part of something bigger. Here they experience the oceanic unity of everything, the interconnectedness of all things, breaking down of boundaries between the person and everything else, without resorting to acts of violence. I am here to offer them peace, a chance to reflect on their own, and if their life ends here, they would have at least spent it in a happy stasis without inflicting harm on others. I am here to offer them a program that inspires deep reverence, or sacredness, coupled with a sense of awe, a sense of the heart opening: infinite love or peace, transcendence of time. Their troubled past fades, haunting them no more as they fall into a tranquil present."

The email stopped there. Both the recipient's address and subject lines were blank.

There was another window open with another email draft;

this one was addressed to some private company's R&D Department, though all it contained was a single line that read: "I'll have them ready by our next meeting. You'll find it's money well spent."

On the desktop were files and folders, most of which were documents and lab reports he skimmed through, catching a few intelligible lines here and there, though the rest may as well have been written in cipher. But among them was a folder labeled "Project Lesath," which contained images as well as a video file.

The images amounted to a hundred or so photos showing patients lying unconscious in bed. The photos were taken in sequence to show the progress of their condition, and scrolling hurriedly through them played the event out in an erratic motion: the patients seemed to twitch with every slight shift in their position. They began to gain weight, swelling in size. Suddenly two sat up, and then a third followed, all three showing a significant loss of body hair, including their eyebrows. The physical change was startling enough, but more disturbing was their identical smile, which they all bore as they stared vacantly at the camera. And while he had seen that same expression in person, something about it being linked to a gradual physical change and remaining ever-present afterwards somehow made it more unsettling.

The video was footage of a patient—perhaps one of the three from the previous photos—with the camera positioned close to his head and a timer rolling in one corner of the screen. The footage sped up and the head began to convulse and shake from side to side; then just as the cheek seemed to bulge out, as if something filled the cavity of the patient's mouth, Greg glanced at the mirror door, and saw it had disappeared, with nothing but a blank wall in its place.

Someone placed a hand on his shoulder and said: "You'd better wake up before you forget how to."

Greg took in his surroundings before he sprang out of the narrow cot, prickling with cold sweat. The capsule bottle fell from his hand and rolled across the wooden floor. His eyes started out as he looked about every which way, frantically searching for something to answer him as to how much time had passed. Sunlight still slanted through the small square window, unchanged in its intensity and hue.

He looked down at the bottle, struck with another question: did he take a dose before blacking out?

Feverishly he snatched the bottle and raised it to the light until the opaque brown glass turned filmy. He counted six capsules. But were there six or seven capsules when he first found the bottle? He scraped his tongue against his teeth, searching for the taste but couldn't find it. The bathroom mirror showed no traces of red on his tongue either. Then again, the capsule might not have broken when he swallowed it—unless that was part of his dream…

Sitting on the edge of the cot, he frowned in concentration as he tapped the bottle against his stubbled chin. No color, no aftertaste, and—recalling that surge of energy that followed his last dose from Nader—no euphoric high. That should have been evidence enough. And yet what if he were wrong? What if he were to take one now and overdose?

He unscrewed the bottle cap, shook out a capsule, and swallowed it dry—not for the strength of evidence, but because between risking an overdose and letting his condition grow worse, he would rather take his chances on the former.

CHAPTER 22

Holden stood behind the partition wall, holding up a bed sheet and listening to the door splinter under the continued assault of the axe. His desperate plan was to hide under cover of dark, anticipating the moment the orderlies managed to enter before ambushing them by throwing the bed sheet on them and then storming past them in the ensuing confusion.

At this point they had managed to break down one of the door panels, through which one of the orderlies reached his hand and unlocked the door only to be impeded by the bed pushed up against the door. And so, grumbling, he picked up the axe to resume his task, intent on breaking down the entire door.

But the axe strikes suddenly ceased, and straining to listen, Holden could almost make out Carver's angry undertones as he addressed the orderlies.

The quiet that ensued lasted long enough that Holden ventured out from behind the wall to peek through the hole the orderlies had made. It offered a limited view of the hallway outside, though it reassured him the orderlies were indeed gone and the coast was clear for now.

He wasted no time making his way back to his room in the staff's quarters, and up until that point, Holden had assumed he had lost no more than a day or two to the induced coma Carver had put him under. But when he opened the door to his former room, and found a blight of black mold colonizing one wall that was absent before, he wondered how long he had been out. Back in the day when he worked under Carver, he had kept his small room clean and tidy, leaving the bathroom door open to let some sunlight into the windowless room. No one had moved in or claimed his room after he had been made an inmate, but the room had remained dry and relatively clean when he last came here to hide Grim—or whoever his lookalike was.

Now, something damp and foul wafted through the bathroom door, which was left ajar, granting a glimpse of its interior and the opaque black stuff smeared large across the white walls in arbitrary strokes.

Holden's first instinct was to step back out and close the door behind. He stood his ground, however, reminding himself that he came here in search of the gun, and that black mold, however hideously metastasized, shouldn't deter him from his task.

But as he looked around the room, he found himself struggling to remember where he had stashed the gun. His mind was still groggy when it came to remembering his last visit, and to help his lagging memory, he sat down at the table, trying to retrace his steps by mirroring his past actions.

At that time, Grim's lookalike lay on the uncovered thin

mattress in a catatonic state, while he, Holden, sat at the table, leaned his head heavily against his hands, and tried to gather his thoughts in the aftermath of the mess he had made of things. If there were ever a silver lining to the whole disaster, it was that it cleared the staff's quarters for the time being, the staff having evacuated along with the inmates to the relative safety and security of the convalescent ward. But it also meant his target was beyond his reach. Worse yet, his only ally was succumbing to the same condition as the inmates, and he hadn't the slightest idea how to help him. His mind blanked out, then it registered the pained moans and teeth chattering coming from Grim's double, who lay curled up on the bare mattress, shivering violently. Holden had to go to a nearby room to fetch a blanket to cover him, but the ill man refused the blanket, and kept irritably throwing it off. Finally, Holden grew frustrated enough to carry him bodily into the bathroom and dump him in the tub, hoping the water would both regulate his temperature and wake him up.

Here, Holden's recollection led him to the bathroom, where he stopped short of pushing back the door after hearing a generous splash of water coming from inside.

Someone was in there.

This was the present, and he was almost certain that Grim's double was anywhere else but here. And yet, someone was splashing about in the filled tub, sending sheets of black speckled water spilling down its side and washing over the tiled floor. The stench was worse with this new disturbance, impregnating the air with a wet, pungent taste.

Holden's instincts now cried out for him to retreat, but he couldn't leave without at least trying the dresser drawers, in case he left the gun there.

He stole nervous glances over his shoulders as he opened one drawer after another, pausing to see if the sound drew any attention. Nothing appeared in the dim doorway, and any noise the drawers made sliding in and out was masked by the sound of water sloshing around the tub and slapping the floor, along with the metallic hiccups of valves turning and the groaning shrieks of metal grinding against metal—or so the latter two sounded to Holden: he had a feeling the bathroom pipes and fixtures were not the likely source of that noise; but neither could he say what would account for them.

He stopped rummaging all of a sudden, thinking he might have heard a voice calling out from the bathroom, but promptly shook it off and continued looking. At last, he recalled the false bottom one of the drawers had, and lifting it now, was relieved to find the pistol was still there.

The magazine was empty; but no, there was one round left in the chamber, rendering the gun almost useless. Or rather, it had spent its purpose then, but could still be put to a different use now without wasting that last round.

"Who are you?" said a voice from the bathroom, cutting clear through the silence now that the noise had died out.

Holden froze, then slowly turned his head towards the bathroom door.

The doorway was empty. Yet there was no mistaking what he had heard, and his eyes focused on the narrow space between door and frame, trying to make out any movement there.

"Who are you?" asked the voice, in the same tone and inflection as before, startling Holden with its familiarity even as he discerned an artificial quality to it, a rasp that made it sound like a recording being played back. A breath of foul stench blew in each time the voice spoke.

Holden faced the bathroom door, fixing his eyes on it as he took a step back.

The voice coughed a little, and the coughs turned into wet hacks that preceded a loud retching noise.

"Who are you?" it demanded between coughs, maintaining the same inflection and clarity, unaffected by the abrasive coughs. Then it stopped, and there was dead silence.

At that point, Holden had his hand on the doorknob; but the silence made him pause, transfixed with confusion. And perhaps that was the intention: to keep him standing there, bewildered enough to drop his guard.

Without thinking, he yanked the door open and ran out, his pounding feet drowning out any noise that might have followed.

Behind him, the door gave a doleful creak as it closed.

In the bright hallway of the convalescent ward, Carver stood speaking with the nurse regarding the missing inmates.

"You say he was last seen where? What about the other one? Don't worry, I've already asked them to guard the front entrance in case they show up—"

The conversation was cut off when Carver detected movement out of the corner of his eye and turned to find a blond inmate standing there, holding a nurse in front of him at knifepoint. The inmate's face was smeared with blood, and he kept his hostage in place by pinning her arm behind her back, while he draped his own arm around her neck, pressing the edge of a knife to her throat. The nurse in his arms bore no discernible marks of injury, though try as she would to remain composed, her glistening eyes still reflected underlying terror.

The sight shocked Carver so that he hardly noticed the second inmate shuffling behind, looking almost as blanched as the captive nurse.

The blond inmate kept his eyes fixed on Carver.

"I've been wanting to talk to you," he said in a guttural voice.

"Of course, son," said Carver gently, lifting his hands in a conciliatory manner. "There's no need to involve anyone in this."

The inmate gave a dry laugh. "You don't get to call the shots here. Like it or not, you get to listen to me now."

"Whatever you like, I'm here to help." Carver took a step forward, eyeing the knife, which had a strange crooked handle, before realizing it was one-half of a pair of scissors.

"Don't move!" shouted the inmate, pointing the knife at him. "I see what you're doing there, and you—" the tip of the blade shifted to indicate the nurse behind Carver— "you stand right where I can see you. One false move and I'll end her life and come after you! Turn around and face the wall! Hands on your head—better yet, get down on your knees—keep your hands up and lie facedown on the floor. Nader!"

The second inmate jumped at the mention of his name, and here Carver recognized him as the dark young man with the injured arm.

"Yeah?" Nader answered uneasily.

"Watch my back. Remember, you're the eyes at the back of my head."

"There's only nurses and patients here, son," said Carver.

“No one is going to—”

“I’m not your goddamn son,” the inmate interrupted vehemently, constricting his grasp in anger, causing his hostage to stand on her toes. She made a small sound as her breath caught. Nader, his back to his partner, turned his head, and murmured something to his friend, which Carver didn’t catch, but was relieved to see the blond inmate respond by relaxing his hold a little.

“You said you wanted to talk to me,” said Carver, addressing the inmate whose name still escaped him. “What did you want to talk about?”

“I don’t want to talk—I want out—I want out of this forsaken nut house. I want out and you’re going to take us to the front door right now.”

“You’re bleeding, my boy. Wouldn’t you rather I look at you first?”

“You stay the hell away from me! You and your fucking staff.” The inmate’s breathing grew quick and hitched, resolving itself into wheezing laughter.

“Do you know what your staff’s been doing?” he asked with a hideous grin, and his tone was enough to distract Nader from his vigil and glance back at his friend as he went on: “You know, right? What they’ve been doing?”

His voice dropped as it broke, and he had to pause to regain control before he spoke in a thicker voice. “I don’t care if my right eye is dangling out if its socket. You’ll take us down—or up, or straight—to whatever doors that lead us outside. If I so much as see one wrong move or someone heading my way: first her blood will be on your hands, and then yours.”

CHAPTER 23

Holden began with the small room just off the dining hall. He knew the orderlies usually sat there for a card game after the inmates had their breakfast and were ushered back to their cells. Sure enough, he found Toby, Roman, and George there, but not Samson. Though Samson was usually inseparable from Toby and Roman, he cared little for cards, and was known to pursue his own form of amusement whenever the other two sat for a game. And while his absence was somewhat of a relief to Holden, not knowing where the largest orderly of the group was right now kept him on edge.

At first, the card players failed to notice him, shuffling cards and mumbling over the hands they'd been dealt. Then Toby glanced at the doorway, found Holden leveling the gun at them, and slowly stood with his arms raised. The other two looked up and soon followed suit. George, who had been leaning back in his chair, almost fell over; Roman's prominent eyes nearly popped out of his skull, and he nervously kept touching the edge of the table, perhaps debating whether to flip it to one side and create some sort of cover for them.

"On the ground!" growled Holden. "Now! All of you, lie down—face to the floor. Hands over your heads, now!"

They obeyed, and Holden, realizing he could not restrain them without risking getting jumped, ordered Toby to stand up, remove his belt, and empty his pockets, placing everything on the table before going back to lying facedown. Holden then ordered Roman to do the same, but also told him to tie Toby's hands with cable ties and bind his ankles together with the leather belt. That achieved, Roman was made to lie back down while Holden checked the security of the cuffs and belt on Toby. Satisfied, he repeated the process, ordering George to empty his pockets and then do unto Roman what he had done to Toby; and checking that Toby was secured, Holden took care of George himself.

From the items the orderlies had placed on the tables, amongst which were a few extra cards, Holden took a set of keys, some cable ties, and a stun gun, which the orderlies had formerly used on him. He knew well enough the staff's uniforms were made with a protective fabric, in case one of the inmates managed to wrest a stun gun from an orderly and tried to use it. But knowing that meant he knew where best to strike.

As he backed out, it occurred to him that he should have taken the orderlies to one of the cells and locked them there rather than leave them restrained in the common room where someone was sure to find and release them. But he had a momentum going, and at this point it was too time consuming to drag them, one after the other, to achieve that. He would just have to work quickly to release the inmates.

Soon he was unlocking the row of doors and giving hurried

orders for the occupants to follow him. To his mild surprise, one cell had been left unlocked, though he soon saw why. Inside, Samson stood with his back to the door, towering over an inmate who cowered in the corner with his arms raised to shield his bruised and bloodied face.

Such scenarios often occurred whenever Carver was away, or was busy making the rounds in the convalescent ward. Not to say he wasn't aware of it, but apart from a few slaps on the wrist, he made no real effort to uproot the problem. Why should he when Samson proved himself too loyal and valuable to be fired? Besides, it was fruitless to try to fix the situation when whatever transpired here—whatever trauma the inmates suffered—would be forgotten as soon as they woke up in the convalescent ward.

Without hesitating, Holden jabbed the back of Samson's neck with the stun gun and brought him to his knees. He kept the giant in that position by holding the muzzle of the barrel flush against his shaved head. The trembling inmate remained cowering, too distraught to understand Holden's words as he tried to talk him into leaving, and Holden had to call out to one of the freed inmates to come in and help him. Two of them ran in and helped the frightened inmate to his feet.

On his way out, the bruised inmate paused to consider Samson; something about the giant, now kneeling and subdued, provoked the inmate, who gave a ragged shout as he began beating Samson. But whether the pounding fists were too weak to have an effect, or whether Samson was too wise to the gun pointed at his head to retaliate, the orderly remained indifferent, and the two inmates had to drag their brother away, who still extended his legs freely in hopes of giving Samson one last kick.

Holden ordered Samson to lie facedown, and then was stumped by the problem of restraining him: all he had were cable ties, which were comically ineffective in Samson's case.

But suddenly a commotion outside drew his attention. Still keeping his gun aimed at Samson, Holden backed into the corridor, and there saw the inmates swarming Toby, Roman, and George, who somehow had managed to free themselves but arrived too late to control the situation: the inmates outnumbered them two to one, and what they lacked in physical strength they made up for in anger and rancor. It was hard to follow what was being done to whom, except one of the orderlies doubled over with his hand to his ear, blood dribbling down his white uniform; another was curled up on the floor, trying to cover his head and avoid the worst of the stomps and kicks; the third seemed to have overpowered an inmate but was soon swamped with others who jumped him.

The scene arrested Holden's attention for a few moments before he whirled around with gun raised in time to stop Samson in his tracks. Where he stood, the orderly filled up the doorway of the cell, and his proximity, as well as the exhilarated grin he wore, as if he could taste what he almost caught—as if this whole situation was merely a game of red light, green light—chilled Holden's blood.

"Back—get back!" Holden barked with the ferocity of a cornered creature. Samson stepped back, still smiling with all his square teeth. Even after the cell door was locked and double locked, Holden could not shake the sinking feeling in the pit of his stomach that it wasn't enough.

But he turned his concern to the rowdy mob and had to physically intervene to control the situation, pulling back one inmate and pushing aside another, all while shouting: "Enough!

I didn't release you all to murder the staff." And seeing he was starting to gain their attention, he went on: "Save your energy. I'll hold them back. You all go down that hallway there and find a stairwell. It'll take you to the lobby. And in case the entrance door is locked—" he took a key out of the ring of keys and tossed it to the inmate who looked to be the most sober of the group.

The inmate caught it, and they all looked up to Holden, as if waiting for him to say more, but he just looked around at the uncertain faces and shouted: "Just go already!"

§

As soon as they stepped out of the elevator, Clark called for everyone to stop.

Carver and Nader looked back at him, the former calm, the latter uncertain.

"Nader," said Clark, tightening his grasp on the nurse. "You go ahead and see if anyone's in the lobby." And turning a sharp look to Carver, he added: "You go with him to make sure he comes back. I don't need to repeat what happens if he doesn't."

The two walked ahead to the lobby, and when they returned, Nader reported that two orderlies were guarding the entrance.

"Get rid of them," said Clark to Carver.

Though Carver had hoped the orderlies stationed near the entrance would show some cunning by remaining out of sight, he now reflected that it didn't matter: even if these two managed to escape the building, they would not be able to travel far thanks to the glass-littered grounds outside; they would get a head start, nothing more, but their bare feet would only carry them so far before they were injured, immobilized, and begging to be picked up again. The image piqued Carver's thirst for retaliation: he wanted badly for those two to suffer for what they put the poor nurse through. It occurred to him then that they might decide to take her with them.

"Release her first and I'll dismiss them," said Carver.

"You don't get to negotiate, old man."

Carver tilted his head back defiantly. "You might threaten to hurt her, but you won't bring yourself to do it—not while she's your bargaining chip. So, I say instead of arriving at a stalemate, we have a quid pro quo—an exchange, if you will. I want her back, alive, safe and unharmed, and for that I'm willing to offer you your freedom for it."

The nurse, as if revived by the promise of her release, lifted her gaze beseechingly to Carver, while Clark continued to stare in disbelief. The situation was no different than it was a few seconds ago, and yet with a sudden dexterous stroke, Carver seemed to have gained the upper hand.

"The orderlies are within shouting distance, you know," went on Carver to reinforce the illusion of being in control of the situation. "I could easily call them here to get you, which puts you at a disadvantage. You might hurt her in the process, but they'll arrest you, and that would be the extent of it. But I'd rather it doesn't come to that. So, I'm giving you a chance: release her to me now, and I'll call off the orderlies."

Clark flashed his slightly crooked teeth in a grin. "You'd like that, wouldn't you? So you could call them here as soon as I let her go. I'll tell you now that I'm only releasing her once I'm outside, some good distance away from the building."

"And what makes you think I'd allow that?"

"You can come with us if you want to keep an eye on her."

Carver laughed at the audacity of the suggestion. "So that you can lead us to an isolated spot and kill us both?"

"Don't give me ideas, old man!"

"That's enough, both of you!" Nader interjected. Neither of them looked at him, but he went on, first addressing Carver: "What if you call off the orderlies and then walk us to the entrance? You and Clark could wait for me while I check to see that the orderlies are really gone and won't come after us."

Then, lowering his voice, he elaborated to Clark: "We can get a good head start as long as no one is nearby. The longer we stay arguing here, the worse it's going to get for us."

To his surprise, neither of them found anything objectionable in his suggestion, and so both agreed to it.

As Carver headed to dismiss the orderlies, he considered instructing them to hide somewhere out of sight but decided against it at the last moment. The broken glass and wire traps would be enough to keep those two from running far.

Not long after, the inmates stood at the entrance, with Clark still maintaining his hold on the nurse as Carver unlocked the glass doors. He swung them open, and in their thin coveralls, the two inmates tensed up like fists against the slap of frigid air. The day was thick with fog, which swallowed the distant trees, and it gladdened the inmates to have a natural cloaking element into which they could disappear.

Carver nervously surveyed the fog but said nothing as he waited by the open doors with Clark while Nader went to check the lobby and nearby rooms and make sure the orderlies were really gone. A frosty breeze fluttered his long white coat. He took it off, wanting to have it ready to drape over the nurse's shoulders as soon as she was released, and tried to pass her a reassuring look.

Clark gave an impatient huff. "He's late. Why is he late?"

Carver, too absorbed in thought to heed the comment, said nothing. His silence troubled Clark, who read in it some insidious intent, like one watching and holding his breath while waiting for a trap to spring on an unwitting prey.

From his position, Clark gazed into the hallway connected to the lobby, and in the dim distance, he could make out two white figures. His blue eyes flared, realization followed by anger; and with sudden force that evoked a cry from the nurse, he dragged her with him through the door as he retreated outside.

Carver made a move to apprehend them but stopped when Clark pressed the sharp edge to the nurse's throat.

"You set us up!"

"I didn't. I—" stammered Carver, snatching confused glances behind him to see what might have triggered the inmate.

"You've got till the count of five to go in and call them off," shouted Clark across the threshold, stepping back and dragging the nurse with him as he counted. "One! Two—"

Something flew by. Clark heard the air whistle but did not at first understand the wet thud, until a spray of blood hit his face. The nurse, who up until now had resisted and held herself apart from him, now slumped against him—dead weight in his arms, surprising him and dragging him down. Something about it all seemed to debone his legs, and he dropped to his knees, still clutching her limp body. His vision was blurred red: one of his eyes had caught a splatter of something.

Another soundless shot flew by, grazing the bridge of his nose. He let go of the nurse and began to crawl on hands and knees towards the only shelter before him, the wide open double doors.

Suddenly, all around him, inmates rushed by, a forest of grey-clad bodies pouring out of the building, running and stumbling and even leaping over him while he scrambled half-blind in the opposite direction, racing against the security shutter, which was being lowered over the entrance.

He managed to reach the doors, managed to get in before the security shutter touched down, completely sealing the front entrance.

CHAPTER 24

"So, what'd you do today?" began the boy uncertainly, looking down at the bright face of the flashlight he held in his hands.

"Nothing much," answered the other with a listless shrug, his eyes similarly cast down at an identical flashlight.

"Did you pass by the donut store?"

"Yeah, but they were out of jelly donuts today."

"Oh. Too bad."

"Yeah," said the other.

After some time had passed, the boy lifted his gaze and stared at his reflection until his mind crossed the threshold where the familiar became alien, and his mirrored reflection was severed from him, becoming its own being. It gave him a wan smile as he sat quiet, turning over the flashlight, trying to think of what to say next.

Greg ghosted the hallway, his lifted hand brushing against the papered walls, fully cloaked in darkness except whenever the light briefly illuminated his wary profile. The corridors were silent and empty; dark, save for the windows that served as beacons, faintly glowing white with mist-addled daylight, marking the end of a corridor, if not a corner bend. Under his bare feet, the cool wooden boards now and then gave a sleepy groan. Outside, the milky fog swirled. Inside, Greg held the sound of the floorboards as evidence that he still had a physical presence, anchored to the here and now.

Rounding a corner, he found a rag with a floral pattern lying on the glossy wooden floor. A delicate fragrance hung in the air, one that dissipated at the slightest disturbance as he stooped down and picked up the piece of cloth, lifting it to the grey light coming from the window behind him. He recognized that ugly pattern of orange, brown, and yellow cabbage-like flowers. And though he well saw what he touched, neither sense explained how a piece of fabric from his childhood's home—or rather, from the kitchen's curtains—had ended up here.

A clean smell wafted from it. He held it closer to his nose and sniffed suspiciously, but found strange comfort in the scent: laundry soap; linen drying on a clothesline; an outdoor breeze drifting through the open window, bearing the fragrance of cut grass and apple orchards—or rather, apple pie dusted with cinnamon sugar...

The more he breathed it in, the more the scent seemed to draw up happy fragments lodged deep within the lines and crannies of his mind, almost blotting out the troubled memories of the same time period. Like balm for his frayed nerves, something about it calmed and settled him; and yet he resisted in some way, narrowing his eyes with uncertainty against this false impression.

No—his childhood kitchen had always had the air of cigarette smoke, of salty food, greasy and overcooked, of coffee always on the heater and poured black. The apple pie was store-bought—a reward for being good, or to assuage some parental guilt.

He saw his mother, after she had pushed a slice of pie towards him, leaning back to blow out smoke, darting an anxious glance towards the kitchen curtains hung over the sink, her face drawn and worried. She would murmur something about wanting to change those curtains, as she would whenever she wanted to distract herself from a stressful situation or any unsolvable issue, before she stubbed the half-smoked cigarette onto a nearby saucer. After all, the curtains were the least of her concerns. Bigger things dogged her, and the curtains were forgotten until she had had a moment to sit at the table and notice them again.

Greg wanted her to look his way, and reached across the table for her empty hand...

The hand that held up the piece of cloth dropped suddenly as Greg looked up to find Grim standing in the grey corridor, one elbow leaned against the table in front of an ornate hallway mirror, regarding him with casual interest. His hair fell to his shoulders, and in the half dark, only the whites of his eyes could be dimly seen: they narrowed in a potential smile, and the orange armband all but gave a coppery luster against his grey sleeve.

Greg regarded him with latent scorn, trying to study the darkened face, seeking the points of resemblance and thinking:

this is what others think I look like.

But before he could discern any features, Grim straightened himself from his leaning position. In synchronous motion, Greg likewise stood up, and the two faced each other.

Grim then turned to step into the denser shadows, and Greg followed.

"I don't blame you," said Greg, addressing the back of Grim's head. "Given the circumstances, I would have done the same."

Grim walked on in silence.

"Self-sacrifice is a noble concept, until it collapses under the right pressure. You need a sort of mania for it to work—to have your head turned by one thing or another. We never tasted that type of unconditional love—not from our parents. I'm sure they were fine people, and under better circumstances, they might have fed me those illusions of stability and sacrifice. But we lived in constant fear. Had to hide who we were. The two of us taking turns—one goes out, the other says in—sharing a single life—a name split between us like an apple. Switch and repeat. I thought it was all behind me. Yet here we are, playing that same elaborate game."

The man walking ahead gave no answer.

Greg considered stopping dead in his tracks and letting Grim walk on without him, just to see whether he would stop as well and turn around. Yet the farther they traveled down the cavernous corridor, the less he could see the figure walking ahead of him, and it became almost unthinkable to stop now and lose sight of him. More so as he began struggling to keep up: for whatever reason, the Skins had started to seize up on him again.

The change began with his extremities: his arms became stiff and his legs grew heavy as scale by scale and plate by plate, the armor raised itself under the Skins' surface, until he moved as if wading in high water.

"But don't think for a minute—" he broke off, gritting his teeth as the Skins' plates had closed over either flank, pressing hard on his inflamed side. Sweat broke out on his brow as he placed a hand over his aching spot and staggered on. "Don't think I'll let this slide. I'll take back what's mine, even if I have to pry it out of your teeth."

Grim melted into the shadows, leaving Greg in the dark and windowless corridor, panting and gritting his teeth as he leaned against the wall, pressing his hand stubbornly against the pain in a futile attempt at mitigating it. He reached for the flashlight and turned it on, carving a small circle of illumination amidst the intense blackness surrounding him.

The pain lingered, but for fear of falling back, he forced himself to put one foot in front of the other. The beam of light bobbed ahead, showing the same papered walls with their dizzy patterns.

Under his hand, his hurting side throbbed, swelling for a pulse, and to subside it, the fingers on his hand split, bifurcated and branched, so that one hand had ten fingers to press down. He knew this without looking; he felt them cleave and divide, new fingers branching from old, until his whole hand blossomed with fingers, and with each sprouting digit, he felt his power grow over the pain, forcing it back into numbness.

But the effort took from him, and he felt a weakening hollow in his stomach. So hungry, he thought with a golden gleam in his eyes as they rolled back, lips parting into a brief grin like a python unhinging its jaws, ready to swallow a deer whole.

Something stalked him. He could hear it behind him, the papery rasp of something rubbing against the wall or ceiling. It was taller than him—tall enough that, as it stood to its full height, the top of its head chafed against the ceiling.

He kept moving, determined not to turn around. To do so was to acknowledge its presence, and to acknowledge it was to invite confrontation—one that he might not walk away from.

Then, something ran in front of him, cutting across the light. It happened in an instant, both the grey blur of limbs he glimpsed and the fluttering laugh that thrilled through the silence before dying out. He had to let go of his side to reach for the screwdriver, holding it with the blade pointed down like an icepick while he scanned the area around him, sweeping the flashlight in frantic lines and arcs, up the wall and across the floor.

His search came up empty, finding nothing in his immediate surroundings. But any relief he would have felt was troubled by doubt; if he stopped looking it will sneak up on him, but he had to slow down, if just to yield to the incessant, gnawing ache that returned and grew worse with each movement.

He tasted blood on his upper lip, absently wiped it, and sniffed to clear his nose. In doing so, he caught a hint of a familiar stench that wafted close before the creature's arms encircled his head, almost closing over his eyes.

But before it constricted its grasp around his skull, his legs went limp, collapsing him to the floor, as if in a faint. It was an instinctive response that served him well: had he jolted or started, his reaction would have communicated itself to the creature, who would have seized up and snared him in an instant; but the suddenness of the drop, along with the pull of his dead weight, allowed him to slip through, leaving the creature to clutch the empty space that he occupied a moment ago.

As he tried to get up, a blow struck his upper back, slamming him facedown to the floor. The strike had a concentrated pressure to it, made by a barbed point-like spear—or perhaps a stinger.

The Skins' raised armor protected him from the stab, and the subsequent one, which came with greater force, determined to break through, if not break his back first. Greg pushed back against the stinger, using his elbows and feet to pull himself from under it, feeling the barb point slowly drag down his back, skidding over the armor's vertebrae plates.

But he hardly gained any ground before more tendrils roped his legs and began to pull him back. And knowing what to expect, Greg twisted his upper body to face the creature, screwdriver drawn and ready to gouge, when a large bony hand clamped over his face and pinned him down.

Again he raised the screwdriver to stab the creature's hand, but felt the makeshift dressing being peeled off his injured foot, followed by a searing pain as the creature poked the gash there. His body tensed into an arch as he tried to sit up and was frustrated in his effort. Unable to kick himself free or withdraw his legs, he curled his feet, and felt warm blood weeping from the wound and down the sole.

Then it stopped, and Greg's muffled scream subsided into labored breathing. His hands were still clenched around the long fingers that caged his head. He opened his eyes and found one of them was able to look through the gaps between the fingers. Though his vision swam in an unfocused haze, the glare of the flashlight illuminated an abstract patch of white drawing close to him, giving the impression of a human-like head. Then his eyes grew wide as the murky shape came into focus, and he saw that it *was* a human head, perfectly symmetrical, looming large and formidable.

The top of the head was bald, smooth, and skull-like; but inches below, from the brow and sides of the head, brown hair grew, crimped and matted, falling long and heavy like curtains that draped the eyes but parted in the middle to expose a small greyish nose and dark, painted lips. The head drew closer still, seeming to peer at him with eyeless interest, until he stuck the screwdriver into the side of its head with a violent force that sank it to the hilt.

Greg was then able to push up the creature's slackened fingers, enough to roll out from under them, kicking off the tendrils that weakly coiled around his calves before staggering to his feet.

CHAPTER 25

Trouble usually slept behind locked doors, thought Holden as he stood by the lab's locked door riffling through a ring of keys. As a custodian, he was never allowed to clean and maintain the lab, even while he mopped the corridors outside, which meant something vital was hidden there.

The door opened to a small and immaculate room with a modest set up: along one wall was a stainless steel sink and shelves of bottles; along another were cabinets and a long table upon which sat a microscope and a stand with a small butane burner.

The outfit was indeed paltry enough that Holden suspected it must have been paid for out of Carver's own pocket, and he was almost disappointed not to be confronted with anything out of the ordinary. Then his eyes fell on the stack of folders sitting on a small desk, and the office chair creaked as he settled into it and opened the first folder.

Somewhere in the room a clock ticked through the silence,

joined by the soft crackle of paper as Holden flipped back and forth between pages, and the arthritic creak of the chair whenever he leaned back, scratching his head with the back of the gun, mumbling a few words and lines as he read them out loud.

He knew the cases were terminal, but he had hoped something in the reports would shed light on their condition, and whether they were truly beyond help after a certain point. The reports however proved useless in that regard: whatever he could glean from them added little to what he himself knew and observed. No surprise, given that Carver was never interested in treating them.

Holden tossed the folder back onto the stack when his eye caught some movement from inside a nearby glass-faced cabinet. The glass was dark brown and, peering inside, Holden found its shelves lined with specimen jars.

He slid open the glass door and picked up one of the several jars to examine it. Like some homemade concoction, each jar had a plain white label marked with illegible scrawl, and was filled with some murky fluid, in which something pale curved unto itself, floating in a delicate cloud of fiber.

Carefully, he unscrewed the jar over the sink and dumped the contents into it, releasing a terrific stench like raw eggs, against which he clasped a hand over his nose and mouth as he peered into the basin for a better look at the specimen.

But the specimen was very much alive: it palpitated, expanding and collapsing, as though it were gasping for air. It began to flop violently, throwing itself with blind fervor against the steel walls of the sink, sometimes sliding, sometimes sticking, its hair-like filaments radiating from all sides. And while the sink's basin was deep, the specimen managed to reach the edge, before Holden slammed it with the thick bottom of the jar, hammering it again and again for good measure. With the same jar he scraped it off the rim, pushing it back into the sink where it lay still, either stunned or dead—or perhaps playing dead like a cockroach.

But dousing it with rubbing alcohol revived it into frantic twitches, and Holden was loath to take his eyes off it while he searched for a lighter or box of matches or anything he could use to burn it.

Stumbling through the door of a small side room, Greg turned around and slammed it shut, leaning against it to steady himself, hands clutching either side of the doorframe and head hanging between them while he caught his breath. Hindered by his foot, a hurried hobble was all that he could manage, not daring to glance back once and see if the creature was close behind.

The wall to his right was taken up by a large window, which would have given him a view of the hallway, except the room was lit by an emergency light, and the window glass reflected its glare, reducing visibility on his side while exposing his position.

He ducked out of view, sitting with his back against the door, listening for any sound or signs of movement from the other side. His gaze edged down to his foot, at the stains between the toes, hesitant to examine it any further, even as it throbbed with pain. Compressing his mouth, he faltered and made a tentative move to turn it over, anticipating a gory sight. Instead he found the wound sealed with some clear substance that had already dried and crusted. He picked at the edges, trying to peel it off, but it stuck to his skin like a scab that was not ready to be removed.

Overhead, the emergency light hummed, and the walls seemed to vibrate in sympathy. But none of it masked what lay behind on the other side, out in the hallway, the soundless creature delicately pressing itself against the door, gathering its weight there as if it were going to force its way in and come spilling through, even as it extended an arm to the windows, as if considering the possibility of breaking through the glass.

The doorknob rattled, locked, and though he couldn't remember locking it himself, for once he was relieved that it was. Even if he leaned against the door to barricade it, his effort was no match for the creature should it try to exert itself. Yet somehow it didn't; it remained outside, butterflied against the walls and window, arms sliding down the glass in slippery squeaks, waiting, pondering, ever patient because it knew it had him trapped and he wasn't going anywhere.

And then it wasn't there, as if it had melted away, lifting, aloft, turning to a wreath of smoke that graced the air. But no, it was somewhere outside, not behind the door but close still. It began to sing, and the hair at the back of his head stood, as if fingers ran there and stirred them.

The song was different, drawing mild and clement, unmarred by wails or shrieks, in a voice so rich and full but with no discernible words, though how little it mattered when there are words without meaning, but not all meanings are conveyed through words; and it brushed over his tired brow, a pleasant, static-like rasp that covered him from crown to sole as it swept away the ache, the troubled thoughts—come, it called, let me take you, don't turn away but come here and let me have you.

He let the singing voice wash over him; there was no avoiding it: stopping his ears did nothing to block it out. Or perhaps he did not want to block it out. Familiar and intimate, it compelled him to rise to his feet, open the door, and step out. But there was no fear of that when inertia stayed his tired limbs, heavy and feverish with spent energy. More than anything he wanted to sink down and sink deep, exhausted as he was to the point where death and sleep seemed equal at that moment, both holding the same sweet promise of oblivion. He closed his eyes, waiting for sleep, which would not come, not while the song, time and again, rose to a shrill cry, which thrilled through him and jolted his nerves like some cruel stimulant. It filed away at his mind, layer by layer, grain by grain, erasing all his coherent thoughts—come, it called, let me wring the fatigue from your body and suck the tiredness from your bones.

I'd rather stay here, he laughed softly, dissembling the compulsion that grew with each passing minute—soon, it would wear him down; soon he would not be able to keep himself from stepping out; already he caught himself about to reach for the door knob to unlock it; already he was slipping away, and had to give his head a shake to regain some clarity. His eyes roved around the bare room in confusion, seeking something but not knowing what.

Then, remembering the capsules, he fished in his breast pocket for the bottle, only to whip his hand out after getting stung by the broken glass.

"No, no, no—" he murmured, each syllable in rapid succession as he pressed his hand over the pocket, heard a brittle crunch, and felt the jagged pieces poking through the fabric. The shock unclouded his mind, and he began to discern a second voice in the hallway—deep and masculine, aligned with the creature's song.

Greg winced as he shifted his position and crawled along the wall towards the window, where he slowly raised himself and peered through the glass, cupping his hands around his eyes to block out the emergency light.

At first the hallway seemed deserted. Then someone approached from the left side in slow deliberate steps, passing by the window. Greg recognized Clark by his profile.

Light from the room spilled into the hallway as Greg opened the door, leaned out to make a grab for Clark, and missed. The creature was nowhere to be seen, though its voice sounded close and clear. Greg extended himself farther out, but Clark remained beyond his reach.

A metal object gleamed in the faint light as it slipped from Clark's hand and dropped to the floor while he went on, placing one foot in front of the other, arms slightly raised, palms up, face uplifted and eyes rolled heavenward, adoringly fixed on the hole in the ceiling whence the song came, answering it with a close imitation in his own dry baritone.

Something dropped from a hole in the ceiling, falling sprawled and spider-like onto Clark's upturned face, covering his eyes and forehead; if he had time to register surprise, it was evident in the way his song had died in his throat, squelched by the sudden touch of the inhuman hand that now held his head, long fingers encircling Clark's head, cleaving through tufts of hair, closing around his skull. And in that brief moment, Clark, with his head tipped back, and his arms half-raised, almost seemed enthralled by the touch he received.

Then the arm that was attached to the spider-like hand, and which seemed to have fallen bonelessly from the ceiling, suddenly became taut as it reeled everything back with it, snatching Clark away with breakneck speed that left no trace of him, save for a fine spray of blood around the mouth of the hole in the ceiling.

CHAPTER 26

For better or worse, the lab's smoke detector failed to react to the billows rising from the charred remains in the sink. Whether it was defective, or whether the batteries needed to be replaced, it was something Holden would have seen to had he been allowed inside the lab. Then again, he would have also noticed the suspect jars lining the cabinet shelves. Then again, Carver likely ignored trivial matters like fire safety, or addressed them by crossing his fingers and hoping for the best.

Holden, emerging from the lab a little wild-eyed and trailing plumes of smoke, wondered what the old goat was up to now. He didn't take five steps before someone crashed into his back; and with the subject of Carver still fresh in his mind, Holden wheeled around, pointing the handgun at the assailant.

The female patient shrank back with a startled look.

"Oh, Millie," Holden sighed, his relief tinged with guilt as he promptly lowered the gun. "Sweetie, you gotta stop crashing into people like that," he went on, thinking her running into him was part of her game. Back when he was part of the staff, Holden was one of her favorite victims to ambush—him and a harrowed old nurse who was assigned to look after her.

"What—no nurse cap today?" he awkwardly teased, trying to lighten the mood, though Millie still seemed a little shaken, casting wary glances at the lowered gun that made Holden want to kick himself for drawing it on her.

"It's okay," he said, raising both hands in a disarming way. "I'm only carrying it for protection. But I'm glad I found you. We need to leave this place."

To his surprise, she seized his empty hand, leading him to a windowed corridor, bright with fluorescent lamps and blue daylight now that the fog had cleared.

They stood at one end of the corridor, staring at the caretaker nurse who lay a few feet away sprawled to one side, her small eyes glazed and unblinking behind the lopsided glasses, her hair and toppled cap soaking up the pool of blood.

Holden, finding a new meaning in the look Millie had given him, said to her: "I didn't do this."

She said nothing, her gaze shifting from him to the body in the corridor with unvoiced sadness.

Holden's concern likewise returned to the caretaker's body, wondering who shot her. He could not begin to calculate how much time had passed since Grim had disappeared, but guessed he must have made it back to headquarters at some point, which meant that by now—were they here already?

Holden stepped forward to investigate the body, but was impeded by Millie, who held him by the elbow and shook her head.

"It's okay," he said, "I just want to have a look."

She murmured something under her breath, and it took him a moment to absorb the word.

"Glass?" he repeated, scanning the floor around the body, until he noticed a fine glitter of shards there, then lifted his gaze to the windows to discern bullet holes in the clear glass.

"Hello?" Nader called out, his voice faintly echoing down the dim and empty corridor. He was almost certain Clark came down this way, and called out again, when someone seized him from behind, and the surprised yelp died behind the hand that clamped over his mouth.

"Quiet! You want it to hear us?"

There was a strange, chlorine-like odor that Nader couldn't place, but he somewhat recognized the voice. He lowered the hand, and turned around to confirm that it was Greg.

"Where the hell have you been?!" Nader almost laughed, stepping back. "You just disappeared. I thought you were—"

The words died off when he noticed Greg's face in the wan light, starker than ever, blood-smeared and drawn, its even features both prominent and carved deeper into their setting, from the dark circles under the eyes to the hollow lines that slanted under them.

Greg meanwhile kept his eyes fixed on the other end of the corridor, seeming to anticipate something that would emerge. Wiping his nose with the back of his hand, he inadvertently brandished the knife he held, which Nader recognized by the oval handle as the same one Clark had with him.

"Come on," Greg urged in an undertone as he took Nader by

the shoulder, "we need to leave now."

"Wait a minute," said Nader, detaching himself from Greg's hand. "I think I saw Clark come down here…"

Greg tore his gaze from the depths of the hallway to regard him with mild surprise, as if just now registering Nader's presence. He looked back again at the dark end of the hallway and seemed to hesitate a moment before answering.

"He's gone."

Nader stared at him in silence, his black eyebrows drawn together in confusion. "Gone—what do you mean gone?" he stammered, thinking that Greg was referring to Clark's unhinged state, exacerbated by some incident that left him blood-splattered and incoherent, slumped against the lobby's shuttered door.

Nader had only been gone for a short interval to check the peripheries of the lobby, and though he heard some distant commotion, the lobby was already shuttered and deserted by the time he ran back. Only Clark was left there, staring vacantly at the floor as he kneeled on all fours, the knife still clutched in one hand. None of it made sense, and try as he would, Nader could not shake Clark out of his stupor any more than coax the blood-splattered knife out of his clenched hands. But while Nader had his back turned trying to operate the nearby control panel to open the shutters, Clark stood up of his own accord and wandered off.

The remembrance absorbed Nader's attention, until he realized Greg was saying something, of which he caught the tail end: "—I couldn't get to him in time. I'm sorry."

It was not an apology for a slip or blunder to be rectified, but a remorseful declaration of something irrevocable.

"I don't understand..." Nader's voice trailed off. Glancing at the knife he went on: "Did he kill himself?"

Greg seemed at a loss for words, then suddenly his head turned towards the dark end of the corridor, as though he had heard something there. Nader himself heard nothing, and there was something half-crazed in the other man's startled reaction.

"Anyway, we can't stay here," said Greg, again taking Nader by the shoulder to lead him away; this time the latter was too dumbstruck to shake him off.

For a while, shock seemed to have dampened his senses; and when he was aware of his surroundings again, Nader found himself standing in the infirmary, surveying the two beds, the green dividing curtains, and to the farther end the small window, smothered with green spruce branches to the point of dimming the room.

The air was still and pristine, and there was a homey aspect to the room that was almost comforting. Even the muffled clatter coming from the floor cabinet as Greg crouched before it and rifled through its contents—even that added another layer of reassurance: no doubt Greg had some purpose in mind or some direction to take and had probably stopped here to gather the necessary items.

Nader sat on the edge of the nearest bed and watched as the older man found and placed one item after another on top of the cabinet—rolls of bandage, gauze swabs, a kidney shaped bowl, a bottle of saline solution, and one of Isopropyl alcohol.

"What are you doing?" he asked as Greg wiped down the knife and placed it in a kidney bowl filled with alcohol.

"Wish we had proper instruments," murmured Greg to himself, seeming not to have heard the question until he said:

"I'm sterilizing it. I need you to perform a small procedure on me."

Thinking this was a sarcastic comeback, and a very poor one, Nader looked at him with a tired expression; but his eyes grew large when he saw the other man had meant what he said.

"Pardon?"

"I need you to operate on me," repeated Greg. "Sounds crazy, I know, but I've thought it through, and it seems the only choice I have. There's this inevitable feeling that if I close my eyes now, I'm as good as gone. Those capsules are losing their effect—not that I have any left—you remember those red capsules? You made me take one. You were right, they did help."

"But what does that have to do—" Nader faltered, afraid to ask. "What do you mean 'operate?'"

"It's not complicated. Look—" Greg pressed two fingers on the right side of his lower abdomen—"I want you to stick the knife here. Just a quick jab like lancing a boil, except on the inside."

"What do you mean a quick jab like lancing a boil!" Nader broke out in a mixture of horror and confusion. "That's your appendix there!"

"See? You know your anatomy. You'd know where to hit—or what to avoid hitting. Trust me, you'll be fine. And don't worry about complications: infection, a little bleeding… we'll sterilize it as best we can and then pack it with all that gauze. I'd still manage to make it all the way down to where I parked the car, and from there one of us could drive to a hospital or even a phone booth and call emergency service."

Nader couldn't help an agitated laugh. "That's the least

of your problems! I mean, look at that thing: it's as big as a carving knife!"

"I know it's not ideal, but it's all we have. Please. Just do this one thing for me. I'd do it myself except I'm afraid I'll pass out or something."

"Greg, listen to me. We can get help. Let's just find a way out."

"And then what?" said Greg with rising impatience. "I won't make a few hundred yards outside the building, let alone down the mountain path. And then what? Are you going to drag me the rest of the way with that one arm of yours?" But seeing he wasn't getting any closer at convincing him, Greg clasped the boy's shoulders and added in a modulated voice: "Listen, you want to go home, don't you? I can help you with that. You do this for me, and I'll smuggle you across the border."

Nader kept his eyes fixed on the wall, though his silence betrayed interest.

"That's what you wanted, isn't it?" Greg went on, with a lopsided smile at having found some bargaining chip against the boy's scruples. "I've got a few hidden spots in my truck where the border patrol won't think to look—unless they're really trying to turn the cabin inside out, which they probably won't. And even if they did, I could throw them off by removing the false bottom of the truck bed and that will satisfy them."

"It isn't about—" began Nader, then paused to clear his throat; it was bad enough his eyes were brimming without his voice failing as well, though a part of him hoped that Greg, seeing him like this, might take pity and relent. "I want to help, but not like this. If we just make it out, we'll find a better way."

"A better way," Greg gently mimicked and gave a parched laugh. His eyes were half-closed now and his speech had slowed to a soft drawl. He left Nader, feeling unutterably tired, and seated himself on the edge of the other bed. "Think it over," he added. "I'll wait here. Just don't take too long. You won't get far on your own. But the two of us? We could help each other."

The silence lasted several minutes while Nader kept a downcast gaze, as though eye contact would inadvertently bind him to an unwanted agreement. He was vaguely aware that Greg had perched himself on the other bed, like a patient waiting for a practitioner to attend to him. He, on the other hand, sat still, afraid to break the silence, all the while trying to think of an alternative solution, and weighing Greg's suggestion against his own misgivings.

Imagine sticking a knife in like that (and he only had one good hand!) when just nicking the wrong spot could bleed him to death. But what if it didn't? Not all stabs are fatal. But with a knife like that, he's just asking to be eviscerated. And his appendix—why his appendix? What did that have to do with his condition? Maybe nothing—maybe he was delusional. Maybe it was another stage in their illness. That had to be it. After all, Clark had the same condition and he seemed to get worse—psychotic even—before he...

Nader lifted a tentative glance at Greg and found him sitting with his arms crossed and his head bowed in a light doze. But his relief was short-lived when Greg's head sank forward and he jerked back awake. Nader dropped his gaze, pretending he was still thinking the matter over, remaining statue still, hoping to inspire the same stillness in his companion. A minute or two later, the sound of soft snoring reached Nader, and he chanced another look at Greg, who had fallen back into a doze. And after pausing to make sure he would not start awake anytime soon, Nader eased himself off the bed and stole out of the room.

CHAPTER 27

Nothing had prepared them for an emergency like this.

After the debacle in the lobby that resulted in one nurse dead and a number of inmates escaping (whether to freedom as they had hoped, or to meet a similar fate, Carver had yet to settle) he expected, as he rushed towards the holding cells, to find something that would explain the catastrophe. Or rather, someone to take the blame for it.

Indeed, when he arrived, Carver found the cell doors all open to empty rooms—all, that is, except for two: Samson was locked up in one, and Toby, Roman, and George shared the other.

Carver's brief surprise returned to livid anger as he dug in his pocket for the master key. And while Samson emerged relatively unharmed, the other three, red and blotched with bruises, had suffered various injuries after failing to control the seething mob of escaped inmates.

To Carver, losing that nurse had been painful enough, but

when coupled with the disaster that followed at its heels, he felt himself akin to the shepherd who rose one morning to find his trusted dog had slept while a wolf had stolen in, slaughtered a ewe, and chased the entire remaining flock off a high cliff. The analogy did not align as neatly to the situation as he would have liked, but in his current mood, and in the absence of other lightning rods to draw the blame, accuracy and fairness hardly mattered. After all, they had grown content and lazy, until someone, recognizing the pattern of their routine, exploited its weakness.

Indeed, nothing had prepared them for an emergency like this.

The doctor watched in apoplectic silence as the orderlies limped out of the cells, but his practical side prevailed upon him to interrogate them later—if there would even be a later—and with a resigned sigh, he motioned Samson to follow him as he started for the convalescent ward to speak with the nurses there about tending to the injured orderlies.

When he reached the ward, he found the nurses there crowding the doorway of the day room. And touching one grey clad shoulder after another, Carver managed to nudge them out of the way, until he saw what had fixed their attention.

The orange-banded inmates, who usually sat in the day room at this hour, now lay in a dead heap near the shattered windows, through which a cool breeze batted the edge of the rolled-up blinds.

Amongst the heap of grey clad bodies were two nurses, and the prequel leading up to this terrible scene played itself out in Carver's mind, starting with the inmates who, one by one, quit their spot and drifted like a swarm of jellyfish towards the windows, pulled by something intangible yet irresistible; they were then joined by the two attending nurses who came to see what had drawn the inmates to the window before someone outside opened fire on the entire group.

Holden was still missing, and so was his new accomplice; under normal circumstances Carver would have said either one was responsible, if not both. But having witnessed the terrible scene at the entrance, Carver knew the assault came from outside—and likely from more than one shooter.

At any rate, no one had the presence of mind to edge to the side of the windows and pull down the cord to lower the blinds so they could check for survivors. Or perhaps no one dared to. After all, nothing had prepared them for an emergency like this.

Greg started awake and looked around, bewildered for a moment by his surroundings, until his eyes fell on the knife soaking in a bowl next to the bottles of alcohol, saline solution, and the packs of bandage and gauze.

"Nader?" he called, looking around the small room.

The last fumes of sleep dissolved once Greg realized how close his brief doze had brought him to the irrevocable sleep that had claimed other inmates. Nader was supposed to keep him from falling asleep—unless the boy saw an opportunity to avoid being coerced into doing something he did not want to do and slipped out as soon as he dozed off.

The idea was ridiculous: Nader might have balked at the idea, though surely he would not leave without waking him up—even if he stepped out to use the bathroom, surely he would not leave him in this state, asleep and unguarded…

"Nader!" Greg called again, unconvinced the boy would abandon him like that.

No answer. And it was soon evident that Nader was gone.

To hell with him then, thought Greg, getting up with the intention of taking matters into his own hands. It was a mistake to think he could rely on others to pull him out of a tight spot. Even if they sympathized, they would sooner walk away than extend a helping hand.

Only this time—for once—he thought it could have been different. In a flare of anger, Greg flung the nearest bottle across the room.

Removing the knife from the bowl, he reclined in bed, undid the zipper, and pulled back the sides to expose the same spot he had pointed out to Nader. His arms remained sleeved, and the rest of him likewise clothed, and seeing his middle exposed like that though a vertical slit evoked a disturbing image of being dissected. Under other circumstances he might have appreciated the association with some morbid delight; now it compromised his already shaky resolve, and with an irritated snarl, he pushed the thought out of his mind.

He began by pressing his hand down his right side, checking for any strange lump or cyst. The distention was mild, but along with the pain that would flare each time he pressed his fingers down, it hindered him from getting an accurate feel. But if he could find it, and pinch it in place, it would be a simple operation—all he had to do was locate it and lance it. He glanced at the sterile gauze and saline solution to remind himself they were close at hand whenever he needed them.

A few inches off the center, where an old appendectomy scar

had long ago healed, he discerned a faint movement—pulsing like a heartbeat.

There it was!—worming along, happy as you please, feeding on him, immobilizing him with sleep and a smiling stupidity… but the drug had cleared his mind and he was wise to its ways.

His mind was clear, his resolve steadfast; but still the razor-edged knife, lustrous from its alcohol bath, remained poised, making a small indentation on the surface of the skin and nothing more.

Perhaps this was not a good idea after all.

He closed his eyes and drew in a few slow breaths. It was either this or fall asleep and wake up like them, he thought. And without opening his eyes, he raised the knife a few inches and brought it down hard.

He threw his head back but somehow managed to bite back a cry. His feet dug into the mattress and his legs arched. A rash of sweat covered him. Then his breathing resumed haltingly, and with one unsquinting eye he glanced down.

The knife's head had sunk in a few inches, and whether because it was not deep enough or he had missed the mark, he still felt the same faint movement under his other hand.

But he was fine—he was fine—no coughing up blood or anything—(something he hadn't considered until now, and the realization struck him with belated horror)—just a brief spell of dizziness to account for this ebbing nausea, nothing more. The room had grown a shade darker—perhaps it was an overcast day outside. His feet were cold, and he extended his legs and slid them under the folded blanket laid out at the foot of the bed. Blood trickled fever-hot down his numb fingers. But he was fine. He could try again. He just needed to lie back and breathe for a moment. In a minute it would be all over. If only the damn thing would stop slipping away…

Descending the stairs with Millie close behind, Holden was surprised to find a young inmate pacing the corridor, seeming intent on going in one direction before changing his mind and turning back. In doing so, he faced Holden, who placed him as the same kid he had met back in the staff's quarters when he was searching his friend, looking every bit as lost and forlorn now as he had been then.

"Still looking for your lost friend?" said Holden by way of greeting.

The boy appeared bewildered, but seemed to have recognized him.

"Everyone's gone," he said, as if the fact baffled him.

"You would too if you knew what's coming," said Holden, pushing past the boy with Millie in tow. "Nasty people outside looking to shoot whatever moves. I won't say no if you want to come with us."

"Wait," said the boy, running in front of Holden to detain him. "My friend needs help."

"Would that be the same friend you were looking for?" asked Holden, continuing to walk, forcing the boy to move at the same pace, albeit backwards.

"What? No—it's someone else. He's got the sleeping sickness, the one you gave me those pills for."

"Wish I could help you, but I'm all out of pills."

"I don't need pills. I just need someone to carry him."

Holden smiled at that. “Maybe you didn’t hear me, boy. There are people posted outside who don’t want any of us to walk out alive. And I can almost guarantee at some point they’ll decide to move in to finish the job. Much as I’d like to help every sorry SOB here, my priority is to get my friend Millie to safety. And I can’t do that while lugging an overweight vegetable.”

“Greg’s not heavy. Even in that strange outfit of his he can’t weigh more than—”

“Strange outfit?” echoed Holden.

“Yeah, like a padded wetsuit or something.”

Holden’s pace slowed to a halt as he considered a moment. “Where’d you say he was?”

“In the infirmary,” the boy answered, and sensing interest went on pleading: “Please, you have to help him. He’d have done the same for me if I were in his place—”

“Yeah—yeah,” said Holden, waving his hand dismissively, “we’re not nominating him for a medal or anything. But first things first—I still need to get Millie to the evac tunnel first. You know where that is? No, of course you don’t. Come on, we’re heading there.”

In his small lab, Carver sat with his head in his hands under a lingering cloud of smoke, while about his feet were strewn the empty and broken remains of sample jars.

None of the orange-banded inmates had survived the shooting, but just the same, they were redundant while he had a few specimens stashed away in the lab. Or so he had thought, until he arrived at the lab and found their remains in the sink.

Five minutes ago, he was piecing together a meticulous plan to take the samples, cut loose, and lay low while he searched for another remote spot to establish himself. Now he had nothing. He could not even muster the energy to even move from his chair.

A nurse ran in and stood in the doorway. Without lifting his head, he knew she had something to report, and was waiting for him to notice her. None of his staff members had ever seen him like this: he always took care to appear the master of any situation—in control, and, with an alchemical touch, able to turn difficulties into opportunities. It mattered little how the nurse saw him now, but her anxious hovering was palpable, and it grew increasingly hard to ignore.

"What," he groaned, letting his hands wipe down his face as he wearily raised his head. It was one of the nurses tasked with taking the injured orderlies to the infirmary to look after them, and at this point he expected she came here to report another casualty, if not some complication regarding the injured men.

But that was not it.

"What?" he asked again, slowly rising to his feet as the nurse again reported what they had found in the infirmary.

CHAPTER 28

"This is it," announced Holden, stopping a few paces down the mouth of the tunnel.

Nader's eyes wandered dubiously over the crude, stone-lined walls but said nothing.

"Not the concrete two-lane affair you were expecting," said Holden, catching that look, "but it's secure, it's hidden, and it'll take us to where we need to go without drawing unwanted attention."

Nader put up his hand in a defensive shrug. "I didn't say anything. Hell, I'm just glad we're not crawling through sewage to get out."

"Don't get ahead of yourself," said Holden. "Anyhow, you two wait here for me while I go and fetch your friend. Millie—" he rested a firm but reassuring hand on her shoulder— "you stay with him. He might not look like much, but he'll look after you. I'm sure you'll do the same. And you—" he clamped his other hand on Nader's shoulder—"Anything happens to her, I'll tan your hide."

Nader gave a timid nod, rubbing the back of his neck as though he already felt something there.

"Alright, now listen," Holden went on. "Some of the staff might turn up here as well, so keep your head down if you can, but don't worry about a few stragglers. At this point they're more like rats jumping ship than following orders." He paused to reflect a moment before adding: "On second thought, if you see them running, you do that: run. Don't wait for me, and don't look back. Just run."

Through the velvet darkness, voices began to seep.

"—set up a blood transfusion. We can't afford to lose him yet. Do we have the same type? Good. Use that then."

Greg felt the hollow of his elbow being swabbed, and opened his eyes in time to focus on the gloved hands inserting a needle there. He felt cold and wanted to sit up, but a nurse gently pushed him down before turning to report this to a surgeon in scrubs and a mask. The surgeon sighed, and with a passing glance at Greg, murmured something to which the nurse nodded before leaving.

With the impression he had been hospitalized elsewhere, and was receiving medical attention, Greg's eyelids drooped, and he almost sank back into unconsciousness, until the surgeon's face, half-hidden and peering down on him, smiled all of a sudden, eyes puckering up behind the rimless glasses in a familiar way.

Greg tried to bolt out of bed only to be detained by Carver, who struggled to keep him down and called for assistance.

The orderlies came in: Toby seized his arms, while Roman tried to grab Greg's legs only to receive a kick to his face that sent him staggering back, hunching over with his hands cupped protectively over his nose. Samson stepped in his place, grabbed each leg by the ankles, and pinned them to the table.

"Samson, you keep his legs secured," demanded Carver, maneuvering around them to take his position. "Hold him down!—Roman, other side—lean on him!"

They held him down as Carver proceeded, removing the knife stuck in Greg's lower abdomen before he staunched the bleeding. Then came the hard part, in which Carver had to pick up the scalpel and continue the procedure.

"Shhh—it's alright now. I'm just finishing what you started," he soothed. "Hold still now. I know—I know—hurts like hell, I know. Alright, there's a good man..."

He went on, not minding the screams that were mingled with profanities, until Greg's outrage collapsed when Carver pushed his hand inside the incision and redoubled force was required to restrain him. Whether his eyes were open or shut, whether he screamed or not, nothing registered to Greg but a relentless torment augmented by the sensation of unseen instruments cutting and probing his entrails, and for which he buckled and strained against the hands that held him.

"I have it, I have it!" Carver suddenly announced, which for Greg preceded the loathing sense of something being pulled out from inside him. Then ease of torment manifested in Greg's facial ligaments as they relaxed and unfurrowed, until he looked—with his upturned face, half-closed eyes, and hungry breaths drawn through parted lips—like a free diver surfacing for his first draft of air after remaining submerged for a long spell.

In his blurred view, he caught a brief glimpse of something Carver held up against the light: slick and lurid with blood, it had the size and shape of a kidney, and seemed attempting to writhe itself out of the doctor's grasp.

Greg felt the restraining pressure subsided as one by one the orderlies gathered about the doctor to attend to it. He tried to sit up, and then, feeling a sharp twinge accompanied by the pressure of his innards pushing against the open wound, collapsed on his back with a groan. Exhausted, all he could make out was the misty impression of their backs as they left the room, crowding around whatever they had extracted, leaving him to breathe away the shock of the invasive procedure.

When he opened his eyes again, Greg found Carver drawing liquid from a small vial with a syringe.

Again, Greg tried to get up, glaring through sunken eyes while he gripped either edge of the gurney to push himself to a sitting position. But the room began to tip and tilt, and while he paused to steady himself, Carver wiped a small patch on his thigh and darted the needle there. Soon a wave of syrupy warmth filled his veins, melting away all the stiffness from his limbs, and with it any resolve of leaving his spot.

"Good, isn't it?" said Carver, smiling with satisfaction as Greg sank back. "Believe it or not, it's not an opioid: no drug test will pick it up—you can't even get addicted to it. But that's just one of its features. It speeds up the body's healing process. My theory is that the larva uses it to keep the host alive and happy, minimizing damage even as they bore and chew their way through them. I've only begun to scratch the surface to its potential. You don't mind my talking while I stitch you up?"

he asked, answering for the pinching tugs Greg felt along the edges of the incision. "Thanks to you, I can still continue my work in that line. So consider this a small token of gratitude, if you like. Old habits die hard, and I can't help but abide by my oath. Or perhaps I've simply grown fond of you, my friend." He shrugged. "Take your pick."

Soon he tied the knot and snipped the silk thread.

"Pray you find the strength to crawl away before the clean-up crew finds you," he went on, setting down his instruments and peeling off the surgical gloves. "I doubt you'll crawl far, though. And judging by their modus operandi, they'd sooner shoot you than keep you alive for questioning. Wouldn't that be a waste? But if it buys me time and throws them off the scent, so much the better," he concluded, tossing the gloves over his shoulder.

He almost walked out of the room then; but the irresistible nag of habit slowed his step as he eyed the cassette player.

Upon reflection that the sound would serve to draw the attention of the intruders—and after a quick survey of the ceiling reassured him there were no exposed vents—Carver went ahead and pressed the play button, and left as an old song warbled sentimentally over a humming chorus and string instruments.

Greg's eyes roved around the room and fell on the knife Carver had extracted from him, which was placed on a roller table to his right. He extended his arm, and his fingertips brushed the edge, but all that did was nudge the table away. He tried reaching for it again, but the table stubbornly remained beyond his reach, and it was an effort to reach for it when it was easier to give in to this delicious weakness.

The song reached a quiet interval in which the music grew

soft while the choir kept humming; it pulled at Greg like a tide going out and he began to drift off; then it dissipated into distant echoes, as if the whole room was suddenly submerged, and he lay with his head turned listlessly to one side, watching the bright landscape of the sunlit room become watery as colors and lines bled into one another.

The room shuddered, hit by a sudden tremor. Through his daze, Greg looked up and found the ceiling tiles overhead sagging under a tremendous weight, a gap forming amidst their warped corners. He felt detached, entombed in a dead calm, even as the ceiling threatened to collapse over him. Nevertheless, he snarled with effort as he fought to raise himself onto his elbows. His legs would not respond, and looking around for something to support him, he found the roller table to his right and began reaching for it.

Another violent tremor shook the room. The roller table shuddered in sympathy and rattled closer. One of the ceiling tiles broke off and came hurtling down past Greg's extended arm just as he managed to catch the edge of the table and pull it close.

A third tremor loosened more tiles or broke off pieces of them. And from the hole in the ceiling, the arms of the creature emerged and spread themselves over Greg in a nightmarish bloom.

Just as he made a grab for the knife, the creature's arms shot towards him.

Everything went black.

CHAPTER 29

Silence had always reigned in this building, but not the silence of emptiness. Even the maddening, monastery-like hush enforced here had been mitigated by sounds incidental to one daily activity or another. And while at first Holden was happy to avoid unnecessary encounters, he began to wonder about everyone's non-appearance. Where was the pandemonium of activity that would typically precede a sudden evacuation: the nurses abandoning their dependents; the orderlies shoving everyone out of the way in a mad rush for the nearest exit? Then again, of the remaining orderlies, more than half of their number were locked up in the cells. Though surely by now they'd be raising hell calling for someone's attention. Were theirs those screams he had heard reverberating faintly when he ascended from the subterranean level to the main building? They never repeated themselves when he stopped to listen. Perhaps it was just his mind filling in those blanks.

The body of the caretaker nurse still lay undisturbed in the same spot. He tried not to look at her, though something about the loose wisps of hair fluttering against the still body drew his attention as he passed her by. So much so that a moment later it occurred to him that he had crossed the corridor without ducking and crawling under the windows to avoid getting shot at. He looked back at the large glass panes but could find no fresh holes or any other signs of shots having been fired.

Silence outside and silence within. Were the snipers still posted outside or had they moved in already? Who or what were they after? He began to wonder whether they would spare him if he stepped forth and identified himself as the insider who had collaborated with one of their agents. What little Grim had communicated to him about them was the equivalent of stolen glimpses, nothing more than hints and intimations; and while Holden knew little of their background, their motives, code of conduct, and intentions, the fact that they were what Grim grinningly referred to as "his cabal" did little to make them sound less sinister.

When he first approached Holden, Grim had vaguely stated he had followed a lead here and needed help infiltrating the place. Assuming Grim was a journalist working an undercover assignment, and not being above getting paid for services rendered, Holden had agreed to assist; and if the wiry bastard happened to publish some name-making piece that exposed the shady circus Carver was running here, so much the better. Smuggling him inside was easy: inmates were never transported through a police car, prison bus, or anything linked to the local authorities or penitentiaries. And the truck that delivered these warm bodies just happened to bring in an extra that evening.

Grim had trusted Holden with his personal belongings, not suspecting or perhaps not caring if Holden chanced to take a peek inside the duffle bag, which held not civilian clothes, but an interesting-looking catsuit, a handgun, and a bottle of red pills. And while they did rouse Holden's curiosity, so long as he kept them with him (thereby controlling access to them) he was not all that worried.

Rather, he was more concerned with strange events that had transpired well before Grim's arrival: inmates that went missing were found injured, unconscious or comatose, and were taken to the convalescent ward, where they eventually woke up, but never entirely recovered. Something about it all bothered Holden, who considered himself a callous, self-interested son-of-a-bitch capable of going about his day, ignoring whatever fresh hell Samson and his crew were visiting on the inmates. He never banked on Carver playing doctor, or making any effort at treating the luckless bastards, who showed signs of early dementia amongst other things; but he drew the line at misleading more healthy inmates towards the same fate, something Carver had orchestrated and all but admitted to.

Grim himself seemed to know more about it than he let on. That was partly his downfall: he could hold a secret, but he could never resist holding it over someone's head. He had asked Holden to smuggle him those red pills on a daily basis, had even disappeared for a while with some of the inmates, yet emerged relatively unharmed. It was only after Holden suspected he knew something and threatened to stop delivering his daily dose that Grim perforce had to bargain again, going as far as to promise closing down operations here. He had claimed that it was more or less his end goal anyway. And whether he was telling the truth or lying to get his way, Holden saw no other way but to agree to it. He wanted to close the place down at any cost—not just to release the inmates, but to shut it down for good; and to that end he was willing to accept the hand that was extended to him, never mind the Mephistophelean figure attached to it.

They never discussed how Grim would go about fulfilling his end of the bargain, though Holden had never imagined it would end in a mass shooting. Either they were picking off their victims at random, or they wanted to eradicate everyone tied to this place; in all likelihood, that included him as well.

When he reached the infirmary, Holden found both beds empty, though the farthest one had its sheet balled up and tossed in one corner. He smoothed it out and found a large bloodstain, neither wet nor quite brown yet. The boy never said his friend was injured, which seemed too crucial a detail to omit.

Holden tossed away the sheet with an exasperated sigh: if the blood wasn't his, this was a waste of time; and there was still an entire building to look through, with unfriendlies closing in.

Just then, a muffled crash sent a terrific shudder reverberating through the floor. Holden looked ceiling-ward in alarm: so tied were his thoughts to Grim's cabal that at first he assumed it was them forcing their way in. Though why would they try to break in from above when it was easier to storm through the main entrance of a defenseless building?

He left the infirmary to check the cause of the commotion when a second, louder crash reported, sounding like someone had dropped a grand piano or something likewise hefty onto the floor above. He paused to listen, half-expecting to hear the sound of boots stomping overhead. No such noise came, but still he crept along the corridors and up the flight of stairs, all the while considering other, more benign explanations for the noise: it might be Carver throwing a tantrum over these series of disasters, flipping tables and knocking over cabinets; or maybe it was the missing fool, locked up somewhere and trying to break out.

He reached the level above, which seemed as deserted as the one below. Just the same, Holden paused before turning corners, listening for footfalls as he made his way through the disquieting silence. Even the gun he held up to ward off any opposition offered diminishing reassurance the farther he traveled.

At last he gained a long hallway, which was situated above the infirmary. The noise should have come from here, yet the floor stretched out, intact and pristine, free from any signs of destruction that would have answered for the crash.

At the other end were double doors with round windows that looked into a defunct operating room. Through those double doors drifted some faint yet sharp sound that Holden first mistook for a feminine voice, crying or keening. But as it went on, it resolved into the shrill sigh of violins.

Holden never liked that room. He stared down the two round windows, which from their distance, seemed to stare back at him.

In his former position, he was tasked with keeping it clean and in proper order, even if it saw little to no use, more so after Carver had set up another room for the same purpose in the subterranean level. "Poor ventilation" had been his reason for abandoning this room, though it was somewhat airy and fairly bright on a clear day, even with the lights off.

Maintaining it, Holden took meticulous care to wipe down all the white surfaces and mop every mint-colored corner, as if expecting it to be put to use in the next half-hour. But it was more in stubborn defiance of the feeling, which he never could shake—a feeling that if he were to turn too soon, he would catch a glimpse of something dashing out the door. He was neither susceptible to superstition, nor was he entirely skeptic: life was too vast, too deep, too full of blindspots to dearly hold on to one stance, and those who sneered at others for being more credulous were mulish fools in their own way.

Something watched him in that room—or beyond it. The feeling was inconsistent—that was the worst of it—he could get used to it if it were ever-present. Once, he had played a tape on the cassette player there just to fill the room with sound and overpower the dreadful loneliness. He nearly jumped out of his skin when a few minutes later the tape suddenly stopped with a loud click. But it was only Carver, who chastised him about disturbing the peace, even if the room was out of the way and almost isolated from the populated sections by its distance.

Along with the soft music that wafted through the air was a faint stench, calling to mind the black-smeared bathroom of his former apartment.

This whole place should be burned down, thought Holden, fetching a long breath before he pushed through the double doors—and almost immediately backed out.

In the center of the room, suspended over a toppled gurney, was a large dark organic mass, seeming to issue from a breach in the ceiling. Holden eyed it for any signs of life, of breathing or sentient twitches, all the while keeping himself shielded behind one of the double doors, ready to bolt at the first signs of threat. Against it, the gun he carried was a joke in terms of protection—he might as well have been carrying a peashooter; but as long as it remained still, he could examine it, though try as he would he could not locate its head, nor discern a mouth or eyes or anything that would answer for that. Then again, part of it was still hidden within the ceiling, while the globular mass visible to him was made of a membrane sac, about six feet across, the look of which called to mind the bulging gullet of a gulper eel or any other serpentine predator that had consumed a prey much larger than its own size and was distended with it.

Behind this swollen belly was a knot of long arms, coiled together to form a twisting, tapering, cone-like shape to that portion. Other stray appendages, amounting to a dozen or so, and varying in size and length, from long tentacles to mere stumps—other stray arms still clung to the edge of the hole in the ceiling, as if the creature had tried to climb back up again. But it seemed like its ungainly bulk kept it trapped in this awkward position, neither able to move on nor vomit up its burden.

The music piece had ended, and seconds later, the cassette recorder gave a loud click as the tape stopped. The creature seemed deaf to the sound. Or rather, not having stirred or breathed in a while, was perhaps dead.

Something black and vicious like crude oil wept from the ceiling and ran in rivulets along the veiny walls of the membrane sac, so strained with its load that it was stretched thin, almost to the point of translucency.

Holden, having taken a few steps into the room, picked up a small piece of debris and threw it at the creature. It bounced off the black mass and fell inconsequentially to the floor.

He looked around and found a scalpel under an upturned tray, and with it he reached up and began to poke the membrane sac. When nothing happened, Holden began slicing down the membrane of the sac, now and then casting an uneasy glance at the wilted appendages, which, out of the corner of his eyes, seemed to twitch back into life; but it was only his slicing and occasional sawing that caused the whole mass to wobble a little and give the impression of movement. The membrane itself turned out to be deceptively flimsy, requiring several incisions through its multiple layers, until at last one broke.

Through the slit, a man's body unfurled and fell out, but not completely: from the waist down, he remained encased within and hammocked by the membrane sac, while his upper half was suspended in the air, head rolled back, and arms sprawled on either side. Black fluid trickled down the half-curled fingers; and from his limp hand slipped something that hit the floor with a dead clatter.

CHAPTER 30

The boy's head dropped forward until his chin touched the clavicle. A secure grip encircled him behind the shoulders and beneath his knees: the boy was small enough to be carried like that. The dim brown interiors of the stale house washed together according to the confused vision afforded to him by unfocused eyes. The man carrying him smelled faintly of cigarettes and faded cologne—a fatherly smell, comforting compared to the stench of decay that filled the house.

An ambulance was waiting for him, and soon he was laid out on a gurney. Inside the ambulance the harsh white light overwhelmed him, and he kept his eyes closed, picking up a few snatches of talk around him.

"...wouldn't have found him if one the neighbors hadn't mentioned they had a son..."

"Yeah, I heard. Didn't someone say they were two?"

"You mean old Cass? She—tends to get her facts mixed up. I wouldn't pay no mind to what she says..."

“Well, it’s not like the parents weren’t their own brand of weird…”

“Show some respect for—” chided the other, catching himself before he let slip the vital word. “Anyhow, poor kid must have hid from them when they broke in and got himself trapped…”

The other gave a low whistle. “That long? No wonder he looks like he’s crawled out of solitary…”

“You’re all heart.”

“Wait a minute—‘them?’ You mean it wasn’t a robbery or some serial killer?”

“Keep your voice down!” hissed the other, glancing down at the boy with concern. “I don’t know the details. But from the looks of it, folks came in from work at the end of the day and—” he paused to clear his throat. “Well, it didn’t seem like they weren’t expecting company…”

Soon they reached the hospital, and the boy was brought out into air and dawn. The blushing blue sky stared down at him as they lifted him up, and he reckoned he was about to fall upwards, fall through the circling birds and disappear into the stratosphere.

Greg’s head tipped back. A reliable grip supported his upper back and legs: he was too hurt to be carried in any other way. Ceiling lights weaved and skimmed over him according to the limited vision afforded by his half-opened eyes. Time folded in the interval between his slow blinks, and when next he opened his eyes, the underground ceiling was replaced by a green canopy of interlacing spruce branches.

He was then lowered and made to lean against a wall of sheltering boulders, which rose in a crest from the sloping ground. The ground itself was rocky, and the air biting cold, and while at first it sharpened him to alertness, with nothing but a wool blanket to cover him, he soon began to shiver, clutching the edges of the blanket to further close it against the chill.

"Here." Holden tossed him a balled-up uniform. "I know those grey pajamas are the last thing you want to see, but it's all I could find, and it's better than nothing."

Greg acknowledged the coveralls with a nod, though he remained huddled in his blanket, reluctant to move just yet and waste whatever meager warmth he had gathered.

Holden scanned the fog-smothered woods surrounding them.

"Listen," he said, crouching now and dropping his voice to a whisper, "I'm gonna go see if Millie and the boy made it out okay. You should be alright here, but we're not yet in the clear. So stay quiet and keep your head down."

Greg gave another nod in response: his throat felt too raw and phlegmy for speech. But when he sensed the other didn't move, he leveled his gaze at Holden, and was met with a look of skeptical concern.

"I'll—" croaked Greg, pausing to clear the liquid rising in the back of his throat. "I'll be okay."

Holden still seemed hesitant, but a moment later he rose to his feet and climbed back up the hillside.

Who's Millie and the boy? wondered Greg.

The thought was a thing separate from him, as though sounding from the distant horizon. His more immediate concern was suppressing the coughs that were building and which he knew would give him hell. But the spasms were beyond his control, and he fell to one side, leaning on his hands to vomit the black stuff, and then collapsing to his elbows as he pressed a hand over the incision site. The stitches tugged like hooks with every heave, and besides the agony he worried the sutures would break. Thankfully there wasn't much in his stomach, and it settled after a few heaves. All the same, he gritted his teeth as he pushed against his elbows and hands and sat back up.

Again he touched the incision, or rather the large wad of gauze taped to his stomach that covered it; clouded as his memory was, he didn't recall Carver had bothered to dress his sutures. Had he the capacity to observe, he would have noted the gauze was clean, whereas most of his body was smeared black. But being drained of heat and energy, he covered himself, tipped his head against the boulder wall, and closed his eyes.

In the distance, a hawk let out a piercing cry. Or so it sounded at first: a hawk's screech has a raspy quality to it, whereas this was closer to a long whistle.

Greg heard it again and opened his eyes, wondering at the sound. Then, from overhead, he heard the crunch of something scraping on top of the boulder, and his heart froze at the thin shriek of an answering whistle: long, loud, and undoubtedly issued by a human.

He sat petrified, not sure why, while the footfalls above made their way down the boulder, and then disappeared into the distance.

All was quiet. Greg tentatively reached for the coveralls, held them in his lap for some time while he listened. And when he heard nothing, he unrolled them, and carefully and methodically slid one leg in. The left leg was easier to dress than the right, and the latter took a little longer while he winced and bit down any grunts of pain. That achieved, and still no sound from anywhere, he leaned against the wall and stood himself to pull up the coveralls and push his arms through the sleeves, even at the risk of dropping from vertigo when he briefly had to let go of his support.

Finally, he eased himself down and draped the blanket over his shoulders, wondering whether he should remain here or venture out while the fog was dense and visibility was low. But then he heard running footsteps somewhere to his distant right, which preceded a black clad figure who darted past him, bounding down the hill. The ground under was shrouded by mist, and phantom-like, the figure's feet never seemed to touch the ground. But there was no mistaking the clatter of the rifle he carried, nor its outline.

Greg inched farther back against the boulders. Besides them, there was nothing to hide him from view. Instead he shrugged the blanket to cover his head like a hood, hoping its muddy color would help blend him with his surroundings. For all that, his camouflage was poor: his right leg remained extended—it hurt to bend it close—while his left was folded at the knee with the left foot tucked under the right thigh.

Now and then, distant sounds drifted to him, the odd snap of a twig or a branch, the crunch of grit—yet never once did they resolve into anything. He began to wonder how much time had passed and how long he would have to remain here—and whether Holden was ever coming back. The shivering had returned, this time a fever chill. The incision began to send shooting pains up his side. He knew this was a bad sign and he needed medical attention, but the trek down the mountain alone would take at least half a day at his pace. Moreover, he could not begin to hope to outrun the riflemen if they spotted him. He suspected they were what Carver had referred to as "the clean-up crew," and if the doctor was speaking the truth, he would do well to avoid them. Even on the slim chance he got lucky weaving between the trees and disappearing in the fog, more of them might be patrolling farther down, and he could not hope to out run them in his state.

So absorbed was he in weighing his chances that he did not register the approaching footsteps until Carver darted in to duck behind the boulders.

The doctor stood there, too preoccupied with catching his breath and stealing glances around the curve of the boulder to notice Greg sitting two feet to his left, staring up at him in surprise.

In his gloved hands, Carver held a jar, about a quart in size, containing a pale, cloudy liquid—and something else, which his gloved hands concealed from full view. He leaned farther out to check whether he was being followed, and was about to dash into the open, when something caught him by the ankle, causing him to lose his balance. The jar flew out of his hand and shattered on a nearby rock.

Carver gave a choked cry and tried to scramble for it, but one of his ankles remained tethered. He glanced over his shoulder, and his eyes all but bulged out in surprise when he found Greg there, fallen to one side, his pale face streaked black, clinging to his leg like a fiend intent on dragging him down to the fiery pit.

Greg himself had acted on impulse, without the slightest idea of what to do with Carver now that he had him. All he knew was that Carver should not be allowed to escape, and to that end he kept his grasp tight, and hoped Holden would arrive any minute now.

But Carver still had one leg free, and with it freely kicked back, going as far as to roll onto his back for better aim. The attack only seemed to anger Greg, who nonetheless clung stubbornly, even as Caver ground his shod heel into Greg's brow, trying to pry him off, and then dashed it down with all the force he could muster.

Somehow Greg caught the foot to block any further kicks, but now had only one hand clasping Carver's ankle, which at any moment could wrest itself from his grasp. The doctor gave up kicking back for now, more intent on reaching his precious sample, and towards it he dragged himself, dragging along Greg, who kept a hold on one ankle and one foot, and whose injured side chaffed against the grit.

Biting back the impulse to scream in agony, Greg wondered where the hell was Holden; and then wondering no more, released Carver's foot, and with his free hand poked his thumb and index finger into the corners of his mouth, and issued a long, loud whistle.

As he whistled again, his one hand hold on the ankle was reduced to clutching the pant leg, which Carver was able to easily shake off as he took off scrambling towards the slimy lump, wriggling in its shallow puddle.

Lifting it in his hands, he looked around for a few frantic moments for any shallow basin to carry it in. And finding none, he lifted his cupped hands like an oyster shell and slid the slippery thing into his gaping mouth. His face flushed livid, his eyes all but bulged from their sockets. He seemed about to choke or throw up. Instead, he compressed his mouth and determinedly swallowed it back. He allowed himself a couple of seconds to breathe, laying his hands on his chest to make sure it rose and fell. Then he turned, and half-ran, half-stumbled downhill, disappearing into the fog.

By the time Greg managed to push himself back up to a sitting position, two black figures ran by, bounding after their target in hot pursuit.

He barely had time to press a hand to his side, when something poked the side of his head, and Greg turned to find the rifle barrel pointed at him.

The rifleman came around and stood in front of him. He wore Skins like Greg once did, except the rifleman was supplied with gloves, boots, and a helmet that hid his face with its smooth, black-tinted shield.

The rifle's muzzle touched Greg's forehead, then pushed against it to tip his head back for the benefit of the rifleman, who wanted to scrutinize his hostage. And having examined the face, lowered the rifle barrel to push back the coveralls a little, inspecting in the sooty stains on his throat and shoulder.

Greg swatted the barrel away, fed up with the rifleman's prodding.

The rifleman almost seemed surprised at this, more so as Greg glared up at him. He trained the rifle on Greg, lowering himself to a kneel, and was close enough that Greg tried to discern a face behind the shield, but saw only a shadow of his face dimly reflected on the smooth black surface of the helmet. He did not hope for mercy, and therefore did not beg it, but tilted his head back to make an easier target of his throat, and waited, maintaining a defiant gaze under lowered lids.

A signaling whistle sounded from somewhere downhill. This time it was different: two short high notes.

The rifleman did not move. Did it matter, though, when

an instant was all it took, a strain of the finger on the trigger and he could rise and turn away before this living target fell dead? It was not the gravity of the act that gave him pause so much as its irrevocability; the target wished it—welcomed it, perhaps—even as a tremble troubled his breathing, the target kept his mouth resolutely shut and his gaze unwavering.

The whistle repeated twice, sounding more urgent now, demanding an answer.

Like a reflex, the rifleman rose up and shouldered his weapon strap. With his back turned to Greg, he pushed up the shield, enough to signal an answering whistle, then lowered it and started downhill.

The fog began to dissipate by the time Holden returned to the boulders. Greg was not there, but he was not far either. Holden managed to track him down and found him wandering down a path, pressing a hand over the incision site, which had grown wet as more blood soaked the dressing.

Wordlessly, he took Greg's left arm and draped it across his shoulders to support him.

Gold flickered in Greg's dark brown eyes as he cast them sunward before squinting against the unbearable glare.

To his left Holden said: "Stay with me now." And then: "You know, I never got your name…"

CPSIA information can be obtained
at www.ICGtesting.com
Printed in the USA
LVHW080516210919
631812LV00008B/21/P